ABOUT THE AUT

Wendy Lewis was b
enjoying the freedo
neighbouring farm.
School for girls, she went on to a varied career as Post Office Clerk, Pub Landlady, Dog Breeder, Farmer, Freelance Journalist and mildly successful poet.

She has had many magazine articles published, and five short stories read on local radio.

Her other three books *THE RELUCTANT FARMER*. *RUSTIC VENDETTA and VILLAGE OF DOGS* have proved very popular.

NEW DOGS IN THE VILLAGE is the sequel to *VILLAGE OF DOGS* and is aimed at 10 year olds and upwards, but both these books are also being enjoyed by dog-loving adults with a sense of humour.

Cover design by John Connor.

NEW DOGS
IN THE
VILLAGE

Wendy Lewis

NEW DOGS
IN THE
VILLAGE
by

WENDY LEWIS

MAZARD
West Sussex

Paperback ISBN 0-9545022-4-8

**Published
by
Mazard
5 Heathfield Gardens
Midhurst
West Sussex
GU29 9HG**

Inspired by Gina's light-hearted love of the absurd and frankly 'dotty', and with thanks to friends in MIDHURST WRITERS' GROUP for their support and encouragement. Also, special thanks to Gregory who unknowingly provided so much inspiration for the more insane exploits in this book.

NEW DOGS IN THE VILLAGE

'That's just what I'm looking for, Peter. Stop the car.'

The woman's voice, coming from the open-topped sports car, roused Patch from where he was dozing on the warm garden path. He raised his head and watched as she got out and walked across to the wrought iron gate which led into his garden.

'Woof,' he said, lazily. Knowing that was what dogs were supposed to do to strangers approaching their territory.

'Yes - it's perfect.' She was staring at him.

'Less of the 'it's'. I'm a 'he', you ignorant human.'

'Just perfect,' she continued: 'Small, ugly and a bit scruffy, short legs, ungainly body and, best of all, the black patch on his shoulder is a perfect match.'

'Oy! Woof, woof, woof!' said Patch. You didn't expect perfect strangers to lean on your gate and hurl insults at you on a warm sunny afternoon…or at any other time for that matter. Really! It was time humans began to realise that dogs could understand their speech. Some human remarks could be deeply hurtful: 'Woof, woof, woof,' he repeated, getting to his feet.

'Do you think he'll bite?' asked the woman, her hand on the gate latch. The man got out of the car and joined her.

'Yes', barked Patch.

'No, I don't think so, he doesn't look very aggressive,' the man replied.

Right, thought Patch. I can do 'aggressive'. He raised the hairs along his back and began to draw back his lips to expose his teeth in a snarl but, while

1

he was concentrating on getting this right, the couple opened the garden gate and walked past him to the front door.

Patch's master, Dad, let the strangers into the house and closed the door in Patch's face, having noticed the ghastly grin that his snarling practice had achieved. He wandered across the lawn re-arranging his face into it's normal, rather mournful expression and lay down again on the grass under the open sitting-room window in time to hear Dad say:

'But he's already been in an advertising film. We had to go to Romania...wouldn't want to go there again, some rather weird things happened.'

That is a massive understatement, thought Patch who still had nightmares filled with bears and werewolves. He gave a shiver, and concentrated on Dad's voice.

'The last one was advertising a dog shampoo, before and after pictures, they had a beautiful black and white Great Dane called Harlequina doing the 'after' pictures,' said Dad.

'But that's who we've booked!' the woman exclaimed.

'NO. NO. A thousand times NO. Not if I have to do the nasty bits that hurt,' Patch whined.

'What a coincidence!' the woman continued: 'But this time all the filming would be in the studio. It's for a new chicken flavoured dog food.'

'YES. YES. A thousand times YES,' Patch barked. Chicken was absolutely his favourite food, next to deer tripes, but you didn't often get that. In fact the only time he had ever had deer tripes was when he had found the carcase of a deer in the woods. It had been killed by his friend Flash, the Greyhound, and

Flash's owner had been so embarrassed, that he had dragged the deer's body into the bushes and tried, not very successfully, to bury it.

'What's all the excitement?' This telepathic voice arriving in Patch's mind came from Dachdan, the Dachshund crossbreed who lived in the village. All dogs can communicate telepathically with each other, when they want to, but at this moment Patch had no wish for Dachdan's sneering voice in his head; he wanted to learn his immediate fate from the group of humans in the sitting room.

'Tell you later,' he snapped, and returned his attention to the man's voice drifting through the window.

'Well, we'll get a contract out to you in the next few days and then be in touch.'

They were leaving. Patch got up and bounded, lumpily, through a flower bed to meet the couple as they came out of the front door.

'Patch! Get off the flowers,' Dad shouted.

That's no way to speak to a famous film star, Patch thought as he tried to greet the two people who were going to feed him chicken. They stepped round his excited wriggles and low jumps and walked down the path. Hmm! Not over-friendly, he thought, gazing after them as they got into their car.

'Who's not friendly? What are you doing?' It was Dachdan's voice in his head again.

'I'm doing another film with your mother,' beamed Patch.

Although she was indeed a beautiful and prize winning Great Dane, Harlequina, in her youth, had had a brief 'fling' with the handsome Dachshund who was Dachdan's father, but she preferred not to be reminded of this.

'It's not fair. You get to meet my mother more often than I do.' Dachdan moaned. He was good at moaning, he rarely did anything else and had an enormous chip on his shoulder about how ugly he was. Everyone agreed that the heavy Great Dane head on a Dachshund body was a most unattractive combination which had resulted, for Dachdan, in a lifetime of bitterness about his appearance: *'I don't think she really loves me,'* he grizzled.

Who does? thought Patch, quickly turning his mind off before this thought could reach Dachdan.

'When are you doing this film?' Dachdan asked.

'I'm not sure. I'll let you know.'

Patch walked down to the garden gate and stuck his nose through the bars to see if he could still see the sports car. There was a vicious snap and a flash of red so close to his nose that he felt the wind ruffle his hair. This was followed by a spate of hysterical barking, a mixture of fright and apologies from the tiny Chihuahua/Corgi crossbreed.

'Patch! I thought it was a monster trying to get me.'

'Chico! You moron! You nearly bit me. Who did you expect to be looking through my garden gate?'

'I wasn't thinking.'

'You never do, that's why you get into so much trouble. Just think, if your teeth had connected with my nose you could have ruined my career in films, and my owner would have been quite justified in suing yours for loss of earnings.'

'What does that mean?'

Patch wasn't sure. It was something he had heard Harlequina mention once when they were filming in Romania.

4

'What did you earn in your last film?' Chico asked.

'A healthy respect for werewolves,' answered Patch: 'I'm doing another film,' he added, casually.

'With werewolves?'

'No. Harlequina, Dachdan's mother.'

'Is she as ugly as him?'

'Oy, you ignorant little squirt,' Dachdan's voice came into both their heads at once: *'My mother is beautiful and famous.'*

'This is true,' said Patch.

Chico's owner was trying to pull him away from the gate.

'I've got to go,' he said: 'What will you earn for this film?'

'Chicken, I hope,' said Patch.

'Maybe…aghh… I will be a film…aghh… star,' Chico's last remark was strangled by his collar as his owner dragged him down the road.

'In your dreams,' said Patch and Dachdan together.

This was probably the first time these two had ever agreed about anything. Chico had never been popular in the village, given as he was to noisy bouts of vicious hysteria.

The next day, Patch and Flash were being walked together on the common. The air smelt fresh in the early morning mist and Flash was on his toes imagining he could see deer and rabbits with every swirl of the mist as it moved in the light breeze. Patch found this lack of attention rendered a proper conversation impossible and had given up trying to tell Flash about being in another film.

'There's one!' Flash vanished. He was soon back: 'Trick of the light,' he said.

'Why don't you wait until I tell you?' Patch asked:

5

'I know I'm not a sight-hound, like you; but I have still retained my sense of smell. At the moment I do not smell deer or rabbits.' He sniffed the damp air: 'But I can smell…sheep?'

'That'll do!' Flash's legs went instantly into top gear. He hadn't gone far ahead before he stopped and asked: 'Which way?'

'Back there.' Patch indicated the way they had come and Flash disappeared into the mist behind them.

Patch had a pretty good idea that humans took a poor view of dogs killing sheep, so he had sent Flash the wrong way. The next bend ahead revealed two stray sheep on the track in front of them.

'You'd better find your dog and get a lead on him,' said Dad to Flash's owner, who set off back the way they had come, calling his dog.

Patch moved towards the sheep: 'Shall I herd them back to the farm?' he asked Dad who, as usual, didn't get the message.

'Come here, Patch. Leave! Bad dog!' He bent and clipped the lead to Patch's collar.

I reckon I am the most mis-understood dog in the village, Patch thought. He was annoyed with Dad. If he had been on his own, really on his own, without Dad and Flash, he reckoned he could have herded those sheep back to the farm and impressed Ankle-shredder, the farm's Lancashire Heeler. Patch thought Ankle-shredder was quite the most beautiful bitch he had ever met. She was normally in charge of herding the cows, but sometimes helped with the sheep. She was good at guarding gateways and keeping the sheep in fields while the tractor drove through, but wasn't so good at herding them because

6

her job with the cows entailed nipping the ankles of the lazy ones to speed them up - it was the cows who had named her - but this was considered a bad thing to do to sheep.

Dad was thumbing a number into his mobile phone: 'Hello Jack, it's Arthur. There are a couple of your sheep, a ewe and a lamb, out here on the main track across the common.' He finished the conversation as Flash's owner came up to them with his dog on a lead.

'You lied to me, Patch,' said Flash, catching sight of the sheep.

'Trick of the wind,' said Patch.

As they walked on past the sheep, the ewe suddenly lunged towards Patch, tossing her head and stamping her front foot, angrily. Patch shied sideways, bumping into Dad's leg.

'What a coward you are, Patch,' said Flash as he whimpered, salivated and pulled at his lead in an effort to reach the lamb. The ewe transferred her anger to Flash, realising he was the more dangerous of the two. She put her head down and charged at him, giving him a nasty bang on his hindquarters as his master dragged him away.

Dogs don't laugh, so all Patch could do was enjoy the little feeling of joy which crept into him as Flash yelped.

'You didn't see that, Patch, all right? You tell anybody about that and…'

'You'll what?' Patch asked.

'I'll'… but the ewe was lining up for another go at him and Flash suddenly needed all his concentration, what with his master pulling one end of him and the ewe pushing the other.

7

At that moment, the farmer's collie arrived like a streak of black and white lightning.

'Out of the way,' he snapped at Flash as he gathered up the two sheep and started driving them back towards the Land Rover and trailer which had parked down the track.

Flash spent the rest of that walk alternately pleading with Patch not to tell anybody that he was attacked by the ewe, and threatening him with how he would bite him if he did. As Flash had to wear a muzzle whenever he was out, after a near lethal attack on Chico, Patch ignored him and pretended to sniff at things along the way. Sometimes Flash could be a real nuisance to a deep-thinking dog.

*

The call from the television advertising company came a week later, asking them to go to the studios.

'We'll have to open a bank account for you if this goes on, Patch,' said Dad.

Patch stared at the steep green bank at the end of the garden and wondered what an account looked like - *open* an account? - maybe it was like a gate. If this was the case, a gate on the bank would allow him to cross the field behind the garden and get straight into the woods. It sounded like a pretty good idea to him. Chicken, and a gate into the woods! What more could a dog wish for? He wagged his stumpy tail and said: 'Woof'.

On the day they were due to set off for the television studio, Patch was feeling slightly grumpy and very hungry because Dad had refused to give him any breakfast.

'No, boy. We want you to eat during the filming, so, no breakfast today.'

'I can do both', Patch whined. He dug in the untidy muddle of blankets in his bed to see if he had overlooked some hidden scraps of food, but all he came up with was half an old, dried-up rawhide chew with pieces of blanket wool stuck to it. He gave it a half-hearted chew, but it was too hard and rough and the wool stuck between his teeth.

Dad put on his coat and took Patch's lead off the hook: 'Come on, boy. Time for you to be famous again.'

Patch slept for most of the journey - riding in the car always sent him to sleep - and woke, feeling ravenous, as they pulled up at the studio.

Harlequina was already there and greeted him like an old friend - they had shared some frightening times together in their last filming session.

In the script for this advertisement Patch was supposed to be an 'ugly-duckling' puppy who, as a consequence of eating new 'Chicken Puppy Chunks' would grow into an amazingly beautiful large dog - played by Harlequina.

Dachdan's voice came faintly into his head: *'Where are you Patch? Are you being walked on the common today?'*

'No. I'm in London, filming with your mother.'

'Hello, Mother,' Dachdan beamed at Harlequina.

'Not now, dear. I'm busy,' she told him.

Oh dear, Patch thought. That's going to put him into an even worse mood than usual.

The actress, who was to pretend to be Patch's mistress in the film, was talking to the camera-man about the best angles to catch the light on her newly coloured hair. She glanced at Patch: 'God forbid I should really own a dog that looked like that,' she

9

muttered under her breath, but Patch heard her.

No breakfast and now insults, this chicken had better be worth it, he thought, giving her a hard stare which she didn't notice.

She picked up a bowl with 'Chicken Puppy Chunks' written on it and placed it on a white cross marked on the floor. Then she took a tin from the cupboard of the fake kitchen set, and held it so that the camera could zoom in on a close-up of the words 'Chicken Puppy Chunks' on the label as she practised smiling at Patch who was hopping up and down on the end of his lead, being restrained by Dad just out of camera-shot.

'Chicken Puppy Chunks. Before sequence. Take One,' the director shouted and someone banged something near the camera.

'Puppy, puppy! Dinner time', called the sweetly smiling actress. Patch looked behind him to see who was being offered this food which he so badly needed. This wasn't fair. But there was no puppy behind him and Dad released him as she opened the can and began to spoon food into the bowl.

With a little push on his behind from Dad, Patch set off towards the bowl. Halfway across the floor his sensitive nose caught a whiff of the food and he slowed down. They said 'chicken', he thought. That smells more like the slurry-pit at Ankle-shredder's farm. He walked slowly up to the bowl and looked at it.

'Cut!' the director shouted: 'That was useless.' He turned to Dad: 'I thought you said he went mad for chicken.'

'I can't understand it. I know he's hungry. I didn't give him any breakfast. Maybe the car journey has made him feel sick. I'll take him outside for a walk for a few minutes.'

'Okay. We'll get on with filming the 'after' sequences with the big dog.

'What's the matter with you, boy? Don't let me down now,' said Dad as they walked in the sunshine: 'You love chicken.'

'That was not chicken. I doubt if that was ever chicken. No puppy should have to face anything like that. I doubt if even a starving dog would eat that. Come to think of it, I am a starving dog and I can't.' His empty tummy rumbled and Dad, as usual, didn't pick up any of this message.

After a few minutes of walking round the car park - very boring, no interesting smells, just fumes and constant noise from the passing London traffic - they returned to the studio just as Harlequina was being led away, having finished her filming.

'Good luck, Patch,' she said: 'Rather you than me; that stuff smells awful, doesn't it? I'm very glad I didn't have to eat any. I can do standing and looking beautiful, but I would hate to have to eat that.'

Why do I always have to do the nasty bits of these adverts, Patch thought, remembering an icy stream in Romania.

'Right!' said the director: 'Let's try again. Chicken Puppy Chunks. Before sequence. Take Two.'

The clapper-boy banged two pieces of wood together in front of the camera, making Patch jump. The actress opened another tin of the dog food and spooned it into the bowl calling: 'Puppy, puppy! Dinner time.'

'Go on boy, please. Lovely chicken,' said Dad, giving him a push. Patch took two slow steps and his tummy rumbled audibly.

'Cut,' said the director… 'No. On second thoughts we'll keep the rumble in. Bit of humour. Okay, Chicken Puppy Chunks. Before sequence. Take Three.' The pieces of wood banged again.

I suppose I've got to do this or we'll be stuck in this horrid place all day, thought Patch. All he wanted now was to get back to the village. A none - too-gentle push from Dad sent him back towards the dreaded bowl. He stood over it, trying not to inhale the smell of the disgusting mess it contained. He still couldn't detect any hint of chicken, but carefully picked out a small chunk. The taste was even worse than the smell, and he dropped it on the floor. His poor deprived tummy rumbled loudly again. The cameraman began to giggle and set the sound recordist off.

'CUT!' the director yelled: 'This is hopeless.'

'Can I suggest something?' Dad asked.

'Please do,' said the director, sarcastically.

'Could you put some pieces of actual chicken in the bowl as well?'

YES! thought Patch, giving Dad a deeply loving look, which he didn't notice.

Somebody was sent off to the canteen to fetch real chicken and Patch began to dribble with anticipation. He could smell the heavenly aroma of warm chicken as it was carried back into the studio, and Dad had difficulty restraining him as they put it into yet another bowl and the actress stood poised with the spoon and a new tin.

'Everybody ready?' asked the director.

'Yes, yes, yes,' said Patch, scrabbling at the floor.

'Chicken Puppy Chunks. Before sequence. Take

Four.'

The clapper-boy banged the two, black and white striped pieces of wood together and Patch didn't even notice the noise. The actress spooned the contents of the can on top of the chicken and set the bowl on the floor calling: 'Puppy, puppy!'… she didn't even get as far as saying 'dinner time' before Patch wrenched the lead out of Dad's hand and, with it trailing behind him, raced across the studio floor to the bowl.

It was there, the chicken was there, but it was covered by the noxious brown muck out of the tin. He frantically burrowed through it to reach the chicken, this was difficult as the bowl was sliding about and 'Chicken Puppy Chunks' were flying in all directions, turning the floor into a morass of sticky slime. The actress was hopping about, trying to get her fearfully expensive Italian shoes out of the way and wiping Puppy Chunk slime off her leg with a tissue. The stuff was proving to be quite a good fake tan remover.

The cameraman was now laughing hysterically.

'CUT! CUT!' screamed the director: 'You. Get hold of your dog. Somebody get this mess cleared up. Take the dog away. We'll break for ten minutes. Somebody get me a coffee.'

A tug on his lead pulled Patch away from the sliding bowl which was now tangled up in a mass of cables at the side of the studio.

'Hey! I was just getting to it,' he beamed at Dad as he was pulled away.

The director's coffee arrived and he took a brandy flask from his pocket and poured half the contents from it into the cup.

After another ten minutes in the car park, during

which the dog bowl was nailed into position on the floor, Dad took Patch back into the studio.

Patch entered reluctantly. It was beginning to dawn on him that there was something about this that he wasn't getting right, but as nobody had explained to him what he was supposed to do, he was at a bit of a loss. He sat at the side of the studio gazing nervously at the director and jumped when he clapped his hands and called the studio to order.

The actress had now borrowed a cheaper pair of shoes and was angry about the fact that she couldn't show off the expensive ones. The cameraman had been 'told off' about giggling and was in a bad mood. Patch found the atmosphere in the studio very intimidating and he was now feeling so hungry that he thought he might even have to eat a piece of 'Chicken Puppy Chunks' before he starved to death. There was real chicken in the bowl, he could smell it.

'Just put a small amount from the tin onto the chicken,' the director told the actress.

She posed with the tin: 'Try to keep these awful shoes out of shot,' she said to the cameraman.

Dad was kneeling on the floor holding tight onto Patch's collar, having unclipped the lead.

'Chicken Puppy Chunks. Before sequence. Take Five.' The clapper-boy banged the pieces of wood together.

Dad pushed Patch to his feet and he began to walk towards the bowl. It smelt all right. He started to trot.

'Puppy, puppy! Dinner time!' called the actress, tossing her gleaming hair and placing half a spoonful from the tin onto the chicken in the bowl. Patch's tummy rumbled loudly as he reached the life-saving meal. Although she had put some of the foul chunks

14

on top of it, he could feel Dad willing him to eat some. Nosing the Puppy Chunks aside, and now too hungry to bother about the slime that was smeared on the chicken, he wolfed down what was in the bowl.

'Cut! Print that. Phew! Thank God! Okay everybody, that's it,' said the director. Somebody cheered.

Dad clipped Patch's lead to his collar and led him to the side of the studio where the stress of the day, and the small quantity of the noxious slime he had had to eat with the chicken, suddenly caught up with him. At the studio exit he began to retch, then was sick all over the expensive Italian shoes that the actress had left by the door.

His last memory, as Dad pulled him outside, was of her horrified screams. He wondered what had happened but had no wish to go back and find out. He just wanted to get home to normality.

*

The following morning, he and Dad were enjoying the freedom and fresh air of a glorious sunny day on the common. Coming towards them were Flash and Frou-Frou who were being walked together. Frou-Frou was a white Standard Poodle who spent a large amount of his time in the show ring winning prestigious prizes, and had a pretty good opinion of himself, but at this moment the three bounded towards each other for a happy greeting.

'Where were you yesterday?' asked Flash.

'London. I told you, I was doing that filming with Dachdan's mother.'

'Oh. The chicken dog food. Was it nice?'

'Filming? What filming?' asked Frou-Frou who thought that he was the only dog in the village famous enough to be filmed: 'Which dog food was this?'

Patch sighed - he really didn't want to recall the horror of yesterday: 'I don't know - something called Mucky Chunks.'

'Do you mean 'Puppy Chunks'?' Frou-Frou asked.

'Probably,' said Patch: 'If they feed that to puppies it won't be long before dogs are extinct.'

'Extinct! What's that?' asked Flash.

Patch had once watched a television programme about extinct animals with Jimmy, Dad and Mum's son: 'It's what happened to the dinosaurs,' he said.

Flash stared at him: 'Were they eating mucky…er I mean, Puppy Chunks?'

'I don't know. Probably,' said Patch.

Frou-Frou had lost interest and was sniffing at the trunk of a silver birch tree. Patch wondered who had passed that way before and left their scent mark.

'What exactly are dinosaurs?' asked Flash: 'I don't recall seeing any.'

Patch gave him a pitying look: 'You don't know much, do you? They were those lizard things.'

'What, those little things that scuttle about on the sand here?'

'I've just seen one,' said Frou-Frou, moving on to the next tree and leaving his own mark.

Flash glanced at him, then back to Patch: 'So those are dinosaurs?'

'Yes, I think so. They used to be huge - but then they got extincted,' said Patch.

'What, kind of shrunk?' Flash said.

'Yes,' said Patch. He was tired of this conversation, mainly because he had reached the end of his knowledge of dinosaurs and wanted to forget the disgusting taste of the 'Puppy Chunks'. Leaving Flash, he trotted over to the first tree Frou-Frou had visited and added his scent mark to the messages left there. His also carried a strong warning against eating 'Puppy Chunks'.

CHAPTER TWO

Patch's family had gone out for the evening, leaving him to guard the house. Jimmy had been very excited and tried to tell Patch all about someone called the Lord of the Rings that Mum and Dad were taking him to see. There weren't any lords in their village as far as Patch knew, but this one seemed to be rather special. He made a mental note to ask Frou Frou if he knew him; he got out of the village more than the other dogs as he was taken to dog shows nearly every weekend.

The kitchen was warm and his bed was so comfortable that he was beginning to drift off to sleep when suddenly a strange voice came into his head.

'Is there anybody there?'

Patch's eyes snapped open. He didn't recognise the thought pattern and wondered if a new dog had come to live in the village.

'Er, yes. I am,' he beamed back.

'What is your name?' the strange voice asked.

Patch decided to use his proper dog name - Patch was just something his people called him.

'He who sits by the fire and thinks,' he said.

'I see. Are you my new spirit guide?'

What on earth was a spirit guide? Patch wondered. He knew brandy was a spirit. He had smelt it and heard Dad telling Jimmy about it. What kind of dog was this? The only dog that had any connection with brandy that he knew about, was a St Bernard. Jimmy had once shown him a picture of one, standing up to its ankles in snow with a barrel of brandy hanging round its neck. Patch had thought this looked pretty uncomfortable, not to mention chilly on the toes. Perhaps this voice he was picking up inside his head was a St. Bernard who had lost its brandy barrel and was looking for a guide to help him find it. That must be it.

'Er - can I help you?' he said: *'I'm shut in at the moment, but if you lost it on the common I could have a look for it tomorrow.'*

There was silence for a few moments. A car drove past the house and an owl hooted in the chestnut tree on the green. Well, it could at least have said thank you, Patch thought, drifting back off to sleep again.

The voice came again: *'Are you related to anybody in this room?'*

'Shouldn't think so; not if you are a St Bernard. Now if you had said Cavalier King Charles, I might have been able to help you,' said Patch whose mother was a Cavalier King Charles Spaniel.

'It's King Charles!' The voice sounded very excited.

Patch decided it was time he had a little more information. Why was this dog so excited about his mother's breed?

'What is your name?' he asked.

'Madam Letitia, your majesty', came the breathless reply.

He wondered if this 'majesty' business was sarcasm, which he had heard about, but hadn't quite mastered yet. 'Madam' must be a registered kennel name, he thought. He was obviously in contact with a pedigree St Bernard. Then he decided that he had better just confirm that this was a St Bernard.

'What breed are you?' he asked.

'Erm - English,' came the answer. The sender

19

sounded puzzled.

'English what?' asked Patch, running through breed names in his mind. English Toy Terrier? English Setter? English Springer Spaniel? *'Are you Old English,'* he asked, suddenly thinking this could be the Old English Sheepdog he had seen in the distance on the common the other day.

'Old! No, I'm not old. I am in the prime of life and at the peak of my powers,' said Madam Letitia.

Patch went quiet. He seemed to have upset this new dog. 'Perfectly reasonable question,' he grumbled to himself. It could look for its own brandy barrel, or whatever it had lost. He snuggled down in his bed.

'Do you have a message for anybody here?' The voice was inside his head again.

Patch sat up once more. It sounded as if there were more dogs there than just the Letitia one. He thought for a moment: *'Well - just, welcome to the village, I suppose,'* he said.

There was another long silence.

'Ivy would like to know if her Albert is there?'

'I think you may have the wrong address,' said Patch.

'Albert passed into spirit two months ago,' said Madam Letitia.

'Well ask him *where it is,'* said Patch.

'Where what is?'

'The barrel of brandy, or spirit, or whatever it is.'

There was another long silence, then: *'Ivy says Albert didn't drink.'*

Didn't drink? Patch remembered television programmes of deserts and dying cows because they couldn't find water.

'Tell Albert he must drink or he will die,' said

20

Patch, helpfully.

'*Albert has died - two months ago.*'

'*Well, that's it then...er, if he died why do you think he is here with me?*' Patch began to feel very uneasy: he had had what he thought was a close encounter with a ghost, once before, and had found the experience very unnerving.

'*He's not here,*' he answered quickly: '*There is absolutely no-one of that name here. I am alone at the moment,*' he glanced nervously round the kitchen.

'*Could you summon Albert, your majesty?*'

'*Definitely not. I positively do not believe in ghosts...why do you keep calling me your majesty?*'

'*Because you said you were King Charles,*' answered Madam Letitia.

'*No! My mother was a King Charles - well, Cavalier King Charles, actually,*' said Patch, a warm memory of his mother filling his thoughts for a moment. He had never met the Bull Terrier who had fathered him, but then his mother had only met him once. He caught a confused, wispy thought from Madam Letitia as she asked Ivy if she and Albert had ever known a Bull Terrier. This bitch is good, thought Patch. She's even picking up thoughts I hadn't meant to send.

'*Where was this Bull Terrier?*' Madam Letitia asked Patch.

'*By the seaside, somewhere. Mother met him on holiday.*'

There was a long silence during which Patch assumed the other dog, Madam Letitia, had lost interest in him. He settled down and began to doze again, half an ear alert for the return of his human family.

21

'Is there anybody there?'

Patch sighed. The telepathic signal was so strong that he assumed this new dog was living quite close to his house on the edge of the village green. At this rate there was a serious risk of it interrupting a lot of his private thoughts and, possibly, his sleep - not to mention his conversations with Ankle-shredder and his other friends in the village, but he didn't really want to be rude to the newcomer.

'Yes,' he said: ' *But I'm rather busy at the moment, please call back another day - or maybe we'll meet on the common when you go for a walk. Goodnight.'*

'Who is that?'

Patch didn't answer; he had just heard the family car pull up outside. He had to do the excited welcoming bit required of all pet dogs on the arrival of their owners. This effort was worth it as it ensured a supply of treats and Patch knew there was some cold chicken in the fridge.

'Do you roam the common at night, your majesty?'

'No. In the morning, usually. Sorry, got to go.' He could hear the key in the lock.

*

The following morning, Patch and Flash were trotting along a path on the common while their owners strolled behind them and talked.

'New person here,' said Patch, sniffing at a footprint in the damp sand of the path.

'Where? Where?' said Flash, staring around them. Flash didn't do much sniffing: 'I'm a sight-hound,' he had explained once, to Patch: 'We find our quarry by sight, you know.' Patch had upset him by suggesting that he should get the vet to give him an eye test, then, after he'd mistaken Chico for a rabbit.

22

Flash hadn't spoken to him for two days before he forgot Patch's remark and resumed friendly relations. Flash had very long legs and a very short memory and attention span but, nowadays, his murderous activities were curtailed by the compulsory wearing of the muzzle.

At that moment, as if on cue, Chico came spinning round the corner ahead of his mistress. He saw Flash, skidded to a halt on the damp path and began to walk very slowly, saying with every step: 'I'm a dog. I'm a dog. I'm a dog.'

Flash stared down his long nose at him, then gave Patch a puzzled look: 'Is he mad?' he asked.

'No, just careful,' Patch replied.

Chico's mistress caught up with him and gathered the little red dog up into her arms.

'Huh!' said Flash: 'She still thinks I'm dangerous, even with this muzzle thing on - I suppose that's something. I do miss the rabbiting, though. Look! A deer!'

Flash was gone, a grey streak across the heather, deaf to his owner's attempts to recall him. Patch wished he had longer legs. The only time he had tried to gallop over the heather he had found it very scratchy on his belly.

Flash's owner set off after him, muttering rude things about darned ex-racing greyhounds.

Patch picked up the 'new-person' scent again and raised his head to peer over the heather that had obscured his view round a bend in the path. Dad said: 'Hello, Letitia,' to the short, middle-aged lady coming towards them.

'Hello, little doggie,' she said, bending to pat Patch on his head. He hated having his head patted. A dog could get serious brain damage from too much head patting. Why couldn't people just sniff him? It was much more informative and unlikely to shorten his life.

Chico's mistress did a quick check to make sure Flash was still out of sight, then put Chico down. He sidled over to Patch.

'I'll stand beside you, if that's all right,' he said: 'After I've barked at this stranger.' Without waiting for an answer, he hurled himself in a flurry of red fur at Letitia, who stepped back in amazement at the red midget's screaming onslaught.

'Goodness!' she cried: 'Will he bite?'

Chico's mistress apologised, quickly put Chico's lead on and walked away down the path. Patch was quite impressed. Although Chico's volatile outbursts usually annoyed him, this seemed like a very good way to ensure that no-one ever patted your head. He tried a tentative, 'woof'.

'Patch! That's not like you,' said Dad.

No, it's not is it, thought Patch and moved away to sniff for any messages left by other dogs on the pine tree at the side of the track.

'You must come to one of my seances,' Letitia gushed to Dad: 'Maybe your wife would like to come. We spoke to King Charles last night, you know.'

Patch stopped sniffing and listened.

'We were trying to contact my friend Ivy's dead husband and we raised King Charles. What do you think of that?'

'It's…er…impressive,' said Dad, nervously.

Patch stared at Letitia. This was the St. Bernard?! He was shocked. At last he had actually found a

24

human who could read dog telepathic thoughts - and it had turned out to be this head-banger. He groaned.

Letitia was still talking: 'Do come. We'd love to have you. Is there anyone you would like to contact?'

'Only the bloke who stole my wallet at King's Cross,' said Dad.

'Is he dead?' asked Letitia.

'He will be if I find him,' was the bitter reply.

Patch remembered the upheaval in his house as the family had tried to remember all the things called credit cards so that they could be cancelled. Humans' lives were so complicated.

'You should get a dog, Letitia,' Dad was saying: 'Something to accompany you on your walks.'

'How about a Cavalier King Charles Spaniel?' Patch beamed the thought directly at her.

Letitia put a hand to her head and her eyes glazed over: 'I'm getting a message,' she said. Patch sat down and stared up at her: 'It's King Charles coming through again,' she said.

Dad looked nervously round for Flash's master, but he was a quarter of a mile away, still calling his dog.

Patch concentrated hard: *'Spaniel,'* he beamed at her, wishing that Flash would come back to witness his power over the odd woman's mind. This could be the first time a dog had got through to a human.

'I'm getting 'spaniel',' she said: 'That's a dog isn't it?'

'There you are, then,' said Dad: 'That's what you should get, a King Charles Spaniel. Well, I must get on. Lovely to talk to you. Come on, Patch.'

Patch trotted after him, well pleased with himself.

He was even more pleased, a few days later, when he saw Madam Letitia walking past the house leading a bouncy, and very pretty, black and white King Charles Spaniel puppy.

The trouble was, he would never be able to prove to any of his friends that he had really been instrumental in her arrival in the village.

CHAPTER THREE

Patch was lying with his chin propped on the edge of his bed, gazing at the 'fridge' door. He was willing it to open and expose the cold cooked chicken currently sitting on the second shelf. His lustful thoughts were so strong that they were picked up by Dachdan in his house across the village green.

'Of course it's cold. Chicken aren't supposed to live in 'fridges', he telepathed to Patch.

'I suppose that's your idea of a joke,' beamed Patch: *'You're only jealous because you never get given chicken.'*

Dachdan didn't answer, and the fridge door didn't open, so Patch began to listen to his human family who were discussing Letitia as they ate breakfast.

'She's been elected to the Parish Council,' said Dad.

'What's the Parish Council?' asked Jimmy.

'A group of local people who decide what would be good for those of us who live here,' answered his father.

As Patch's real name was 'He who sits by the fire and thinks' and, as it didn't look as though he was going to get any chicken for a while, he decided to think about Madame Letitia and the Parish Council. A glimmer of an idea was slowly forming in his mind. He was still thinking about Madam Letitia and her forthcoming influence on the village residents later on, when Dad walked him across the green and tied him up outside the shop, next to Dachdan whose person was inside. Patch was so lost in thought that he didn't acknowledge Dachdan's presence.

'What's the matter with you, then? Do I smell, or

27

something?' Dachdan asked.

'You do a bit, have they been bathing you again?'

Dachdan ignored this - he didn't want to think about bathing. If he could have, he would have reported his people to the RSPCA for forcing this indignity on him.

'Sorry. I was thinking,' said Patch.

'About what? Not cold chickens again.'

'No. You know that head-banging Madam Letitia human?'

'The one with the pretty little King Charles Spaniel puppy? I fancy her, you know.'

'She's much too young for you. No. I have found that I can make Madam Letitia pick up my thoughts sometimes, if I beam them in a very concentrated form. Well, it seems that she has some influence over what happens to the inhabitants of this village now that she has joined this Parish Council thing. So I thought...'

'No more short leg discrimination,' Dachdan butted in.

'What?' Patch stared at him.

'Equal rights for dogs with short legs.'

'Equal with what?'

Dachdan had to think about this: 'Well, we should be allowed to go into the shop like everyone else. Look at that sign on the shop door.'

The sign he was looking at was definitely a picture of a dog very like Dachdan, long body, short legs, but not quite so ugly, and it had a red cross superimposed on it.

'I never get taken into the shop,' said Patch.

'I'm not surprised,' sneered Dachdan: 'Humans are a bit fussy about smells. What have you rolled in this time? It's not bad by the way. Nearly as good as the decomposing rabbit you found the other week.' Dachdan sniffed at the side of Patch's neck.

'Yes, though I say it myself, that did make me very attractive. Ankle-shredder spent a long time sniffing me. Most exciting.' The hairs on the back of his neck prickled as he remembered the scene.

'She's got no taste,' said Dachdan, jealously: 'I bet she sniffed you with her eyes shut.'

'Careful,' Patch growled: 'At least my parents were more of a match than yours, well for size anyway.'

Before Dachdan could retaliate, Flash turned up with his owner who tied him firmly to a ring in the shop wall.

'What are you lot doing then?' he asked, his eyes scanning the shop roof in case the squirrel he had once seen there should come back.

'Patch thinks he can put thoughts into a human mind,' Dachdan said.

'Well, get him to make my person take this muzzle off, then.'

'He can't. The dog warden said you would have to wear it for the rest of your life after you nearly killed that Chico,' said Dachdan, nastily.

'How long is that, then?' asked Flash.

'Not long if I had my way,' said Dachdan.

'He's in a bad mood this morning,' said Flash to Patch.

'He's got a complex about his legs,' said Patch.

'What legs?' said Flash, bending down and peering under Dachdan. Dachdan bit his leg. Flash yelped: 'That wasn't fair. I can't bite you back.'

'Tough!' said Dachdan, suddenly feeling a little less gloomy.

29

Patch intervened, he didn't really like violence, you never knew how it might spread and involve onlookers: 'This Madam Letitia,' he said. Flash lay down and started to lick his damaged leg: 'This Madam Letitia, well, she's…are you listening Flash?'

'Yes,' said Flash, studying his leg to see if it was going to bleed.

'She might be in a position to influence things that happen in the village and, as I have told Dachdan, I can sometimes put thoughts into her mind.' Patch sat up straighter and thought he probably looked impressive. He was the only dog he knew who could communicate with a human being.

Flash didn't seem impressed. He flexed his ankle. It didn't appear to be broken. He glared at Dachdan through narrowed eyes. Dachdan lifted his top lip, exposing gleaming white fangs. The rest of Dachdan looked pretty odd but he did have the most amazingly beautiful teeth and Patch was momentarily distracted.

'What are you staring at?' asked Dachdan, aggressively.

'Nothing. As I was trying to tell Flash, I might be able to make things happen in this village. Nice things - for us dogs.'

'I know what this village needs.' Flash was suddenly paying attention: 'One of those places that rabbits live in.'

'Holes,' said Patch: 'Rabbit holes.'

'Warrens,' said Dachdan, scathingly: 'Why do I have to spend my life amongst such ignoramuses. If my mother hadn't been so careless I could have been a champion Great Dane.'

30

'All right then - warrens,' said Flash: 'That's what this village needs. Warrens on that big flat field next to my house.'

Patch thought this was a good idea. He had never caught a rabbit due to the fact that he was nearly as deficient in the leg department as Dachdan, but at least the rabbits would be more interesting to look at than that boring, close-mown sea of grass. Mind you, humans seemed to find it interesting; men from the village - including Dad - would stand studying it, stamping on it and talking about it for ages. Sometimes they watered it, then, the minute the parched grass began to grow, they rushed out and mowed it. Yes, a rabbit warren would definitely provide more enjoyment.

'That is the humans' playground. That's where they do their cricket. Rabbits would get in the way,' said Dachdan.

'Well then, I could earn their gratitude by getting rid of them…if my muzzle was off,' said Flash.

'Not much point in starting it, then,' said Patch.

Flash's master came out of the shop and untied his lead. Flash limped as he was led away.

'So dramatic! I didn't bite him that hard. There wasn't even any blood,' sneered Dachdan: 'Now Patch, if you really can influence what humans do with us we need to give the matter some serious thought.'

'She's coming now,' said Patch, as Letitia came out of her cottage across the green with her new puppy. The little black and white King Charles Spaniel bounced across the grass on the end of her new red lead.

'Nice,' said Dachdan. His eyes glued to the puppy.

31

'My mother was one of those,' said Patch: 'Well, the Cavalier variety.'

'Pity her beauty managed a total bypass where you were concerned. Were your brothers and sisters as ugly as you?'

'It was you who won the prize for the funniest looking dog at last year's dog show,' Patch reminded him. Then wished he hadn't lowered himself to Dachdan's level of insults...after all he himself had come third.

Dachdan didn't really hear him because he was straining at his lead to touch noses with the new puppy; she was wagging and wriggling at both of the older dogs. Letitia picked her up and went into the shop carrying her. The door swung shut behind them leaving Patch and Dachdan staring at the picture of a dachshund covered with a red cross. They waited for Letitia to be escorted out by an outraged shop owner.... but nothing happened.

'That's age discrimination as well as short leg discrimination,' muttered Dachdan.

Patch was thinking again: 'You know there should be some way that we dogs could actually meet each other regularly. I know we can talk telepthically but it's not the same as being within sniffing distance.'

'Yes. We're being denied our natural rights,' Dachdan sighed, head up, trying to catch the last vestiges of the sweet scent the puppy had left in the air.

'Jimmy goes to the Youth Club in the village hall where he meets all his friends,' Patch continued.

'He's a human.'

'Yes, but what about a Dog Club?' said Patch.

Dachdan finally dragged his eyes away from the

shop door and looked at him: 'A Dog Club?'

'My mother used to say she missed the Dog Club when she was rearing us puppies. I wonder if I could put the idea into Madam Letitia's mind for the next Parish Council meeting.'

'You mean all of us get together in the village hall? I've been there once when I was a puppy - something called a jumble sale. Lots of human legs and feet. I was trodden on twice and the floor is slippery.'

'Mmm,' said Patch and went back to thinking again: 'I've got it!' he said a few moments later: 'What about the barn at Ankle-shredder's farm? That's a lovely place, full of interesting smells, gorgeous mucky straw to roll in...and mice to hunt.'

Dachdan brightened up: 'That sounds better. Who's going to ask Ankle-shredder? She's a bit fussy who goes on her farm since Chico drove the cow into the slurry pit.'

'We won't have to ask her. This thought will come from Madam Letitia's mind - if I can put it there. This had better be a secret between you and me,' said Patch, suddenly realising that making Ankle-shredder angry was not a good idea now that she had decided he was her favourite dog. Ankle-shredder's mission in life seemed to be trying to make gloomy dogs happier, and since Patch's near nervous breakdown over meeting the Big Cat in the woods, she had transferred her affection from the permanently gloomy Dachdan, to Patch. In one of his more philosophical moments Patch had wondered if this was, for her, some way of compensating for all the cows she had made unhappy by chasing them and nipping their ankles. This did deeply worry the cows for a few seconds, as she was so quick that they

33

couldn't see where she was in time to take avoiding action. All they got was a fleeting glimpse of something black and noisy, followed by a sharp pain in the fetlock.

*

For the next few days, Patch tried to imagine a way of getting the thought of having a Dog Club in the village into Madame Letitia's mind, then suddenly the opportunity arose.

'Parish Council meeting tonight,' said Dad as he came home from work.

Patch pricked up his ears, well one and a half ears; the other one had never really worked right to the tip which dropped over making him appear slightly unbalanced. When he was a puppy, Jimmy had taped the floppy ear into a straight position on his head, but when he had finally managed to pull the tape off, plus a considerable amount of hair, the ear had flopped over again and Jimmy had given up.

Parish Council meeting! This was it! He watched Dad eat a quick tea and when he set off for the village hall, Patch went into his bed and pretended to be asleep; he needed to concentrate. At first this was nearly impossible as Mum was clattering dishes and Jimmy was talking to her, but eventually they both went upstairs to the bathroom.

Patch put his chin on the edge of his bed and tried to reach Madam Letitia's mind.

'Madam Letitia, are you receiving me?'

'Is that you, Patch?' It was Dachdan.

'Go away,' snapped Patch: *'I'm trying to reach Madam Letitia.'*

'Sorry.'

'Who told me to go away?' asked Letitia, looking

around her: 'I thought this was a friendly village.'

The people gathered in the village hall looked at each other in puzzlement, then assured Letitia that no-one wanted her to go away - on the contrary they were all delighted to have her with them: 'And your dear little dog,' said one man. Letitia had brought her puppy with her because it wouldn't stop barking and whining when she went out and the neighbours complained.

Patch tried again: *'Madam Letitia, are you there?'*

Letitia suddenly realised that the voice was saying *Madam* Letitia. The village people called her Letitia. This must be a contact from the 'other side', she thought. She decided to keep quiet and listen to the voice in her head while the village discussed whether they could afford a new bus-shelter.

'Madam Letitia - it's King Charles here.' Patch had decided to stay in the character she had created for him as it was the one which seemed to impress her most.

'Majesty!' she breathed, and quickly turned it into a slight cough, looking apologetically at her neighbour. She concentrated hard and tried to communicate by thought: *'What is it you wish to tell me, your Majesty?'* she sent.

Patch sat up. Got her! he thought, and quickly stopped that thought from transmitting.

The Parish Council had decided they couldn't afford a new bus shelter after all, and Flash's person had offered to repair the old one, to much applause from those gathered there. He volunteered for a lot of these sort of things to try to mitigate the damage and stress that Flash's actions caused in the village.

Patch was frantically trying to decide exactly what

35

he and Dachdan wanted - neither of them had ever been to a dog club. He thought they just wanted somewhere where all the village dogs could meet and sniff and bark (and maybe growl, if Dachdan was being particularly annoying).

'I got that!' said Dachdan.

'Get out of my head. I'm busy. I've made contact.'

'Sorry.'

'Madam Letitia, I understand you have a new puppy of a breed named after me.'

Letitia looked at the people around her in the hall. They had moved on to discussing the paucity of street lighting in the village. She moved a hand down quietly to stroke her puppy under the chair. This was a mistake as it had been asleep and, waking in a strange place, it wanted to investigate its new surroundings. It was a minute or two before she could settle it down again.

Patch thought he'd lost her. Then their thoughts clashed in mid-transfer as they both sent messages at once.

'Yes I - Madam - have - Letitia - a dear - are you there?- little puppy.'

'Not very good at this, are you?' It was Dachdan sneering again.

'All right, you do it.' Patch flopped down in his bed in a very disgruntled manner.

There was a silence while Dachdan tried, but he was not projecting on the same wavelength as Patch and none of his thoughts reached Madam Letitia, which was just as well because he'd sent: *'Oy, you with the gorgeous new puppy - what about letting us get together sometime?'*

'You are really not very good with people, are

you?' Patch sighed: *'Don't you ever watch your humans? Try it, you might learn something about them - for a start, they do not think like dogs.'*

'That's their loss, then.'

'Dachdan...'

'All right, all right. I'm going. It's all a stupid idea anyway...you do it.'

Heavy footsteps sounded on the landing as Jimmy ran from the bathroom to his bedroom: 'Mum! Can Patch come up for a bit?'

No, thought Patch, burying himself in his blanket and pretending to be asleep.

'I'll see if he wants to,' said Mum.

'Are you there, your Majesty?'

He concentrated hard: *'Yes. Madam Letitia you should start a club in the village for....'* The blanket was pulled off his head and Mum said: 'Patch, do you want to go upstairs with Jimmy. Come on, boy.'

Patch groaned, turned his head away from the sudden intrusion of light and shut his eyes again.

'Patch is asleep,' Mum called back up the stairs: 'You can read for a little while if you like.'

Letitia, in the village hall, having lost her connection to King Charles, was trying to think what kind of a club she might start. Knitting, perhaps, or patchwork quilting, she was good at sewing and was currently making a little quilted coat for her puppy. She was thinking about her puppy when Patch came through again: *'As I was saying, why don't you start a club for dogs?'*

'What can dogs do, your Majesty?' Letitia was frowning in puzzlement. The lady sitting next to her asked if she was all right.

'Yes. Yes, dear,' she said: 'I was just thinking

about er…a club for dogs?'

'Oh. What a marvellous idea,' said the lady: 'An Agility and Obedience club.' She was looking at Flash's owner as she spoke the word 'obedience'.

The Parish Council meeting had reached the stage of 'Any other business' on the agenda. Letitia's neighbour raised her hand and said: 'Letitia has just had this super idea that we should start an Agility Club for dogs. I know this is not Parish Council business, but if anyone would like to discuss this with us after the meeting, please come over.'

Unaware of the turn things had suddenly taken at the Village Hall, Patch was still pondering Madam Letitia's last question about what dogs can do. There was so much that they could do - he didn't really know where to start. He tried to answer her.

'Well, they can seek out and dig up old bones, and hear the really high pitched squeaks from mice…'

'Mice!' Madam Letitia's mind squeaked, a little lower than that of a shrew, but still high enough to make Patch jump: *'I don't like mice, your Majesty. We have decided on an Agility and Obedience Club. Thank you for your suggestion.'*

An Agility and Obedience club? thought Patch, not really sure what this meant, but becoming uncomfortably aware that it might not quite be what he and Dachdan had had in mind when they first discussed all this. Dachdan picked up this thought with mingled horror and satisfaction. Horror that there now seemed a chance that he might become involved in Agility, and satisfaction that Patch hadn't been quite as clever as he thought he was: *'Huh!'* he said: *'Made a right pig's ear of that, didn't you?'*

'How did pigs' ears come into this?' Patch asked.

This was all moving too fast and getting too complicated for him.

'*Just an expression my person uses sometimes. You see I do listen to them...humans. You can't be trusted to do anything properly, can you? My mother told me about the mess you made over the dog food advert.*' said Dachdan.

'*I'm going to sleep now,*' said Patch... and he did.

CHAPTER FOUR

'That new puppy came down to the farm this morning,' said Ankle-shredder, looking across the green

She and Dachdan, Flash and Patch were lying on the grass in front of the pub while their owners drank and chatted. Patch followed her gaze and watched as Letitia crossed the village green towards them, her puppy bounding along beside her.

'Come and join us, Letitia,' said Dad.

Dachdan had risen to his feet and was straining towards the new puppy, trying to touch noses. She suddenly seemed overwhelmed by the number of dogs around her and rolled over on her back, then as Dachdan did sniff her, she leapt up yelping with fright and hid behind Letitia, who picked her up and cuddled her.

'Dachdan's face has that effect on me, too,' Patch muttered.

'Don't be horrid, Patch,' said Ankle-shredder: 'He can't help being ugly.'

'That's two of you. Have you got anything rude to say about me, Flash?' asked Dachdan.

'What? What? Did you just see that cat? The short-tailed one from next door to you Patch. I could have had the rest of it before it jumped over that wall if only I had been off the lead.' The cat's lack of tail length was down to an earlier near miss by Flash. His eyes were fixed on a garden wall across the green and he whimpered slightly with frustration.

Dachdan was still staring at him, waiting for an answer to his question. He sighed: 'Apparently not. I suppose I should be thankful for small mercies.'

'Cheer up,' said Ankle-shredder: 'My news might make you happier. As I was saying; that puppy came down to the farm, and the humans who were with it were all talking to my person about using our barn for an Agility Club.'

'You idiot, Patch! Now look what you've done,' said Dachdan.

'What's he talking about?' Ankle-shredder asked Patch.

'There it is again!' Flash screeched, wrenching at the lead in his owner's hand and causing him to spill most of his beer, as the cat jumped down off the wall and slipped under the garden gate of the house next door. He cursed his dog and tied the end of the lead to his chair leg. Flash lay down again, his slanting eyes fixed on the gate across the green.

'What is your name?' Ankle-shredder asked the puppy as it watched them, wide-eyed, from Letitia's lap.

'Nell - I think,' said the puppy: 'I'm just learning things. It's either Nell or Sit or, maybe, Heel.'

'You really are very young, aren't you?' said Ankle-shredder: 'I think you can safely rely on your name being Nell, the other two mean something else which you will learn in time.'

That time was to come sooner than any of them expected and they would all begin to learn things which they had quite happily managed without in their lives so far.

That afternoon, Dad was talking to Mum about Letitia and her new venture into the world of dogs, when the word 'Agility' caught Patch's ear - he was only half listening.

'My friend at school takes his dog to Agility

Shows,' said Jimmy: 'Can we take Patch?'

'Well, not for a while, darling. We'll have to see how well he does at the classes,' said Mum.

A little bunch of hairs at the base of Patch's spine rose as a slight shiver of apprehension trickled through his body. He got up and went to his water bowl and lapped, messily, for a long time to calm his mind, then walked over to the back door leaving a trail of drips across the kitchen floor. Mum let him out into the garden and reached for the mop.

He wandered down the path to the gate and saw Letitia and her puppy coming up the road on his side of the green. Nell wagged her tail madly and pulled her mistress over to Patch's gate.

'I'm going to school, Patch…what is school?'

'It's where Jimmy goes every day. I thought it was for humans.'

'Oh. My name *is* Nell, by the way. My person says I was named after a friend of someone called King Charles.'

'I don't have a friend called Nell,' said Patch, thinking of his alter ego with Madam Letitia.

'You do now,' wriggled the puppy, touching noses with him through the bars of the gate: 'I'll see you at the school, I think everyone's going,' she said as she was pulled away.

School? Patch sat down to try and work out what this information meant. A blackbird who had been happily singing in the top branches of the apple tree, suddenly flew off screeching a warning to all the other neighbourhood birds as the short-tailed cat clawed its way rapidly up into the lower branches, whiskers and bottom jaw twitching.

I wish I could fly, thought Patch.

'You'll need to be able to from what I can gather.' Dachdan's thoughts arrived in Patch's head.

'Oh? Now what?' Patch beamed back, grumpily.

'This Agility thing. That mad woman with the gorgeous puppy has just been round to my house. You should hear what they are going to try to make us do in the name of agility and obedience. Not only that, but at the end of the year we're going to have to take a test, something to do with the Kennel Club, to prove we are good citizens.'

'What's a citizen? The Kennel Club? That's what Frou Frou is always talking about - showing and that. We're not going to be show dogs, are we?' Patch asked in alarm.

'No. It's all about running and jumping and sitting still,' said Dachdan.

'Sounds pretty weird to me,' said Patch.

'Most un-doglike behaviour,' said Dachdan: 'I vote we start a resistance group.'

'How would that work?' All these new ideas were crowding into Patch's brain and making his head hurt.

'Well, we'd just resist; like, sit down and protest.'

'I thought that sitting still was one of the things we would have to do. Protest how...you mean bark and growl?' The idea of barking and growling as a group rather appealed to Patch. He stood up and did his loudest barking and a truly ferocious growl at the cat, who was still in the apple tree. I think I might be quite good at this 'protesting' thing, he thought, until the cat stared down at him.

'You are pathetic,' it hissed: 'You don't scare me.'

'Come down here and say that,' Patch growled, refusing to be put off.

43

'What are you doing, Patch?' Dachdan asked.

'Oh, just putting that annoying cat in it's place.'

'I heard you from my house. Quite impressive.' This was the nicest thing Dachdan had ever said to Patch who, after the initial warm glow from the compliment, began to wonder if there was something Dachdan wanted from him.

There was.

'That gorgeous puppy was heading your way - can you put in a good word for me?' said Dachdan.

'Too late. She's gone,' said Patch. He didn't quite add a gleeful 'so there', but he would like to have done. Then, for good measure he added: *'And she said she was my friend; her name's Nell, by the way.'*

Dachdan didn't answer, but sent out waves of grumpiness that affected several dogs in the village for a minute or two. Chico snapped at his owner, who shut him in the kitchen. Ankle-shredder nipped so hard at the ankle of one of the cows she was driving from the milking parlour to the field, that it leapt into a gallop, forcing the slow-moving cows ahead of it to get momentarily jammed in the field gateway. Patch found himself giving such a menacing snarl at the cat that it decided, after all, the best route home was an impressive leap from the apple tree to the garden wall. Even Frou-Frou, who was usually above such things, growled at his owner who was snipping away at the curly white hairs that formed the pom-pom on the end of his tail. She began to worry that there might be something wrong with him that could affect his chances in the show ring the following day.

The kitchen door opened and Jimmy came out carrying a football: 'Patch, stop making all that noise,' he shouted, and kicked the ball across the garden, yelling 'GOAL!' as it shot between the apple tree and a large flower pot.

Me noisy? thought Patch.

Dad opened the kitchen window and said: 'Take that out onto the green, Jimmy. I've told you about kicking footballs in the garden.'

A little piece of the Dachdan wave of grumpiness still lingered in the atmosphere, prompting Patch to lunge, angrily at the football as it trickled past him on its way from the makeshift goal, but his teeth slid off the firm surface.

'LEAVE!' Jimmy shouted, making him jump. Then: 'SIT!'

'Sit, yourself,' Patch grumbled, walking back towards the kitchen door.

'Dad - he won't sit,' Jimmy shouted.

'Go and play on the green,' called Dad, letting Patch back into the house.

As Patch wandered over to his bed, Dad said: 'You have my full permission to chase that cat out of the garden, I'm fed up with the mess it makes in the flower beds, but don't do a 'Flash' and start biting bits off it.'

Patch gave a half wag of his tail and flopped down on his blanket and began to daydream about biting bits off cats. He made a mental note to ask Flash what he had done with the end of the cat's tail, next time they met.

*

The next time he saw Flash was on the fateful day of the first meeting of the Agility and Obedience Club at Dean Manor Farm, where Ankle-shredder lived.

When he realised where they were going, Patch

was in two minds. One mind was excited at the prospect of meeting Ankle-shredder, with whom he was secretly, deeply in love, and the other mind was absolutely dreading the idea of having to be agile. He thought he could probably manage obedience as this was already in his nature but he was not built for agility and was well aware of the fact. I'd need longer legs for a start, he thought...and a more streamlined body.

The owners and their dogs all gathered in the barn which had been freshly floored with new wood chips to make a soft surface. These smelled delightfully of pine and silver birch but still retained enough sawdust to get up Patch's nose, making him sneeze and his eyes itch. He complained about this and Flash told him to stop moaning.

'It's all right for you, your face is further away from the floor,' Patch grumbled.

Flash was feeling grumpy as well because he had been made to wear his muzzle in case he mistook Chico for a rabbit again. Chico was hiding behind his mistress's legs, barking with fright with his mouth closed so that Flash wouldn't hear him. This wasn't very successful because everyone turned to see where the odd noise was coming from; it was a cross between a strangled grunt and the sound of a dog being sick.

'Why is he doing that?' Flash asked, lowering his head and peering at Chico over his muzzle.

'Don't look at him, you're making him worse,' said Dachdan. His eyes were on Nell, the puppy, as she bounced in, attached by her lead to Letitia: 'Cor, get an eyeful of that,' he muttered to Patch.

'I've got an eyeful of sawdust,' said Patch, rubbing

his eye with a paw covered in more sawdust, which made it worse. He sneezed again.

The farmer, Ankle-shredder's owner, noticed this and fetched a hose with which he sprayed the area, damping down the sawdust which improved matters.

'Hello, Patch. What do you think of the equipment then? This is going to be fun.' Ankle-shredder's eyes were shining with excitement.

Patch's tail wagged uncontrollably as he took in her dark beauty, enlivened by the tan markings on her shining black coat. He wasn't sure what she meant by 'equipment' but she was gazing at some small, brightly coloured fences placed around the barn: 'Very nice,' he said, carefully.

'I can jump all those,' she said: 'I had a practice, earlier.'

'Jump!' said Patch, appalled: 'Is that what they are going to make us do. Jump fences? That's what horses do, not dogs.'

'And that's an A frame,' she said, looking at two boards propped together: 'You go up one side and down the other.'

'I don't,' said Patch, with a shudder: 'I can see absolutely no reason for doing that when you could walk round or under it; going over the top leads nowhere.'

'And this is the tunnel,' said Ankle-shredder, turning to a long, curved, collapsible plastic pipe: 'You run through here.'

'Why?' asked Patch.

'Oh Patch, you just do. You must try to enjoy this. In fact I think Dachdan told me this was all your idea so why are you looking so miserable about it?'

'I'm not going to have any more ideas, ever,' said

47

Patch: 'This one has come out all wrong. The only good thing about it is that it has made you happy,' he added, but his beloved had got tired of his negative attitude and was trying to calm Chico down before he hyperventilated himself into a coma.

Letitia clapped her hands together and announced that they were about to start and that their trainer for the day would be Mick, a police dog-handler.

'Police, did she say?' asked Flash, nervously. It had been the police who'd insisted on him wearing a muzzle after he'd nearly killed Chico: 'I think I'll go home now.'

'I'll come too,' said Patch, and they both pulled on their leads, trying to drag their owners towards the barn door. They weren't strong enough and both men said: 'Sit!' at the same time. Neither dog sat, they were too tense.

Mick looked across at them: 'Say it as if you mean it,' he said, coming over to them. Taking Patch's lead from Dad he marched towards the centre of the barn to demonstrate, pulling an unwilling Patch beside him: 'SIT!' he shouted. Patch tried to get back to Dad: 'SIT! Mick repeated, pulling Patch's head up and dropping a heavy hand on his bottom. Patch was scared and tried to bite the hand. He was never quite sure afterwards what had happened, but the next second he was upside-down on his back with his feet in the air and Mick's hand on his chest, pinning him down: 'I will not take aggression from any dog, however small,' said Mick, as he allowed a shivering Patch to regain his feet.

'Patch isn't aggressive. If you want to see aggression, come over here,' Ankle-shredder barked at Mick, who didn't understand, or even glance at her.

Patch was returned to Dad who was nearly as shocked as he was: 'It's all right, boy. I know you were only scared. Maybe this obedience thing is not suitable for all dogs.'

'Too true. Let's go home.' Patch pulled towards the door again, but Dad pulled him back.

Mick was now giving them all a lecture on curbing the first signs of aggression in their dogs, and all the dogs were looking more than a little nervous, except Nell who wasn't quite sure what 'aggression' meant, and Ankle-shredder who was still angry at the way Patch had been treated. She was glaring at Mick and silently lifting her top lip to expose shining white teeth every time he raised his voice.

'We'll start with the smallest dogs first,' said Mick: 'Then we can increase the height of the jumps as the dogs get larger.'

'Will I get larger, Patch?' asked Nell, who was sitting beside him.

'Well, yes...er no, well, yes, but not because of jumping fences.' He tried to concentrate on Nell and quell the trembles still running across his skin under his coat which was standing away from his body. Dad noticed this and ran a hand over him to flatten it, but the hairs sprang back.

'Your coat's all 'stary'. Are you scared or angry?' Nell asked.

'Um, angry, definitely angry,' said Patch and found that with uttering this statement he began to regain control over his body.

He stood up and shook himself and his coat flattened into its normal smooth state. He played with this new feeling of anger in his mind, finding it

49

changed his whole body. He stood taller, arched his neck, and a steely look came into his eyes as he directed his gaze towards Mick, who wasn't looking - but Nell was: 'You're magnificent when you're angry,' she whispered in his ear, her large brown eyes shining. Patch felt himself grow another two centimetres; nobody had ever called him 'magnificent' before.

'Let's start with the little fellow I have already met,' said Mick, rubbing his hand at the memory and making the assembled humans laugh: 'What is his breeding?'

'The mother was a Cavalier King Charles spaniel, as to the father, that's anyone's guess,' said Dad, causing more laughter from the owners.

So much for loyalty. His own person was turning him into a joke. It was at this point that Patch began to seriously revise his opinion of humans, there was coming a glimmering realisation that dogs were actually more loyal and probably more intelligent than people. He looked round the barn with this new thought in his mind and began to count the ways that the assembled dogs actually, to a large degree, controlled and manipulated their humans. This profound train of thought was interrupted by a tug on his collar as Dad led him towards the first jump. He put the thought away until such time as he was lying quietly in bed and could pursue it thoroughly.

'Stay angry, Patch,' Nell said, as he was led away. He began to trot beside Dad with his head held high, which was a good idea anyway because it kept the sawdust out of his eyes.

'Patch looks different,' said Dachdan to Flash.

'Does he?' said Flash, who never noticed anything

unless it was small and furry and running away from him.

Patch and Dad stopped beside Mick: 'Right. I want you to just lead him over that first jump. You run beside the jump and say 'OVER' as he jumps it,' he said.

'Come on, boy!' said Dad. Patch snorted with derision at the ten centimetre high pole ahead of him and flew over it at such a pace that Dad got left behind and forgot to say 'OVER'.

'Very good, but you didn't give him the command,' said Mick: 'Do it again.'

'Keep up, Dad,' said Patch, as they faced the first fence again. This time they co-ordinated their efforts.

'Keep going!' shouted Mick: 'Go over all the others.' Patch was galloping and flying the little fences so impressively that the other dogs wanted to join in. Ankle-shredder, never one to hold her tongue, led the barking, joined rapidly by Chico who finally had a proper excuse to bark hysterically.

'What's he chasing? Where is it?' asked Flash, his head swivelling, eyes ranging over all of the barn ahead of Patch.

'Oh, shut up,' Dachdan groaned, moving away from him; he was seriously disgruntled by all the adulation Patch was receiving from Nell and Ankle-shredder, especially Nell whose high-pitched puppy bark had enthusiastically joined Ankle-shredder's staccato delivery and Chico's manic screams.

Two fences before the end Patch began to run out of steam, but he forced himself on and he and Dad both pulled up panting, after the last jump. Patch stood, sides heaving and his tongue hanging out. Dad bent over with his hands on his knees trying to catch his breath. The humans were all clapping their hands together which Patch knew was a sign of approval.

'Praise him. Praise your dog. Well done,' Mick said, smiling.

'Yes, come on, praise me - and don't forget I like chicken,' Patch panted.

Dad duly praised him and gave him a small liver flavoured treat out of a packet. It wasn't chicken but it wasn't bad. The two of them moved back to their place near the barn wall where Dad sat down heavily on a straw bale.

'Phoof!' said Patch, lying down on the soft wood chips.

'Yours next,' said Mick, pointing at Chico and his owner: 'Let's see if we can get his legs to work as fast as his mouth - Chico was still barking although all the other dogs had quietened down.

Flash was staring up into the rafters of the barn, trying to find the mouse he had decided Patch had been chasing. Unable to see it he looked down again just as Chico ran past him towards the second jump. His one-track brain registered 'something small and furry' as his legs propelled him into a lethal lunge towards Chico. He was stopped by his lead, still firmly held by his owner, but Chico began to scream again and developed such a turn of speed that he wrenched the lead out of his owner's hand and, ignoring the rest of the jumps, disappeared out of the barn door into the darkness, his lead trailing behind him. After a few seconds the screaming stopped.

'Where did it go?' said Flash.

'That wasn't an 'it', it was Chico again, you idiot,' said Dachdan: 'You're in trouble now.'

Flash didn't answer - he was too busy trying to

avoid the end of his lead with which his owner was attempting to thrash him.

'I didn't - arrchch - know - arrchch - did I? Arrchch!' Flash eventually managed to choke through his strangling collar.

Dad had handed Patch's lead to Dachdan's owner and gone out with several other people to look for Chico. Mick was having a serious talk with Flash's person about keeping his 'lethal weapon' under control. Flash's person looked as if he would like to go home and cry. Preferably without his dog which, in an ideal scenario, he would have dropped over the parapet of the bridge into the deepest part of the river on the way back to his house.

'Excellent idea,' Patch muttered, catching this last thought.

Mick went to the barn door and looked out at the flickering torches around the farm as people searched for the little red dog in the dairy, hay barn and surrounding hedgerows.

'Let me go. I know this farm better than anyone. I'll find him,' Ankle-shredder barked. The farmer unclipped her lead and she shot out of the barn, her nose to the ground, picking up Chico's terrified fear-scent immediately. She followed it round to the feed shed where there were two large galvanised iron bins containing corn; both lids were closed, but out of one of them was hanging the muddy end of Chico's lead. He had climbed up some straw bales beside the bin, which had been open, and had slipped in, knocking the lid shut, trapping him and, fortunately, his lead which although it was nearly strangling him, was just keeping his head above the corn, otherwise he would have sunk to the bottom and suffocated.

'Here bark! Here bark! Here bark!' Ankle-shredder stood on the bales calling the farmer who knew her well enough to know she had found something.

Soon, the lid was lifted and Chico was hauled out, semi-conscious from fright and lack of air.

'He's in shock,' the farmer said: 'Better give him some brandy.' But Chico's mistress thought she had better let the vet have a look at him and she drove off to the surgery as everyone trooped back to the barn.

'Well done, Annie,' said Patch as Ankle-shredder trotted back in looking very pleased with herself.

'Good job I was here,' she said: 'Nobody else seemed to know what to do.'

'You are clever,' said Nell, admiringly.

'And so modest,' said Dachdan. His sarcasm went right over Ankle-shredder's head, she didn't 'do' irony and had a true northerners approach to life. She always said what she thought and if others took offence that was their problem, she wasn't worried. Patch, who had stood up to congratulate her, found that all the stress and recent activity had gone to his legs which suddenly felt very tired. He lay down again.

Mick moved back to the centre of the barn: 'Right! As Patch is turning into our star pupil, let's see him go over the A frame.'

Dad stood up: 'Come on, old lad. Let's see what you can do.'

Patch got up again, rather stiffly, trying to remember which piece of apparatus Ankle-shredder had called the 'A frame.' Dad led him towards the two boards propped together; these rose high into the air, peaking about a metre above Patch's head. As they reached this contraption he stared up the steep slope and felt his already weak knees weaken further.

'No! I can't go up there. I can't stand heights and something's happened to my legs.' It really had. As he spoke these words his legs collapsed leaving him flat on the ground, and flat on the ground had never felt so good. He hugged the woodchip floor and tried not to whine. Dad pulled him to his feet and led him to the base of the A frame. Patch began to tremble and Mick walked over to them.

'Just put his paws on the first ridge. Show him it's solid and safe, then lead him gently up.'

Dad placed Patch's front paws on the bottom of the board. Patch froze, listening to the faint scratching noises his toenails made on the wood as he trembled.

'Now take him forward. Offer him a treat.'

Dad pulled on the lead, holding out a liver flavoured treat in front of Patch's nose.

'Come on, Patch. Hurry up. We want a go.' Ankle-shredder barked impatiently, eager to show off her agility skills.

He stretched forward for the treat but Dad moved it just out of reach. He took one step, then another which took both his hind feet onto the board. This doubled the scratching sounds.

'Ooh! Patch do be careful, don't fall off,' Nell squeaked.

'I don't mind falling off - it's the landing that bothers me,' said Patch, trying to control his shaking limbs as he took another step, then one more.

Dad was so pleased that he gave him the treat as Patch was in mid-stride. By now he was trembling so much, and vertigo had taken over to such an extent that as he reached the last few centimetres for the treat he knocked it out of Dad's hand, and in trying to catch it he overbalanced and fell off the side of the frame, scraping his front leg on the way down and yelping as he landed on his side.

'Poor Patch. That's twice he has been hurt this evening,' said Nell.

Letitia was thinking: *'Oh dear. This was all my idea.'*

Patch caught the thought: *'No. It was mine, but somehow the idea got lost in the translation.'*

'Is that you, your Maj.....?' Letitia stopped and looked round, wondering if anyone had heard her, but they were all watching Patch as he limped back to the side of the barn with Dad, who inspected his leg for fractures and finding nothing more serious than a slight graze, allowed Patch to lie down again. He began to lick his sore leg better.

'Will you be able to go for walks again?' asked Nell.

'Probably,' said Patch, spitting out a few detached hairs. He looked up again in time to see Dachdan being led across towards Mick. This should be good, he thought, watching as Dachdan held back, going as slowly as he could without actually pulling on the lead.

'Try him over that first jump,' said Mick.

'He could walk over it at that height,' said Ankle-shredder with derision....and that was exactly what Dachdan did - walked over it with his front feet and brought his back end over with a sort of ungainly hop.

'Can you make him move a little faster. Get some impetus going then he'll have to jump it,' said Mick.

Dachdan's owner tried, he tried really hard, doing little short encouraging running steps, half bending towards his dog and trying to tempt him on with a small piece of liver held out in front of him. Dachdan's speed increased not one whit and, so hard was his owner concentrating on his dog's short legs, that he didn't notice the wing of the next low jump and tripped over it, measuring his length on the woodchip floor and dropping the lead.

'Thank goodness that's over,' said Dachdan, trotting quite smartly back to the side of the barn, where he was caught by Letitia and led back towards his owner who was trying to brush woodchips and sawdust off his clothes.

'Let go of me, madam,' said Dachdan, pulling back on the lead until his collar almost came off over his ears.

'You are being naughty,' said Nell, trotting along happily on the other side of Letitia.

Dachdan found being told off by Nell, a mere puppy, rather embarrassing: 'I'm just making a stand for the whole of dogdom,' he said: 'This entire evening is against nature and demeaning.' But he did stop pulling back because the collar was hurting the back of his ears and Letitia didn't seem prepared to slow down. She handed the lead back to his owner.

'I don't really think jumping is his scene. Those legs are too short on that long-wheel-base body,' said Mick.

'I knew it! Here we go again with the insults,' said Dachdan who was especially sensitive after a lifetime of human jokes about his looks: 'If he comes near me I'm going to bite him.'

'Yes. Do it!' barked Ankle-shredder.

'I wouldn't,' said Patch, who could still feel Mick's iron grip on him and the growing bruise on his back where he'd hit the floor.

'Try the tunnel - that should appeal to his Dachshund blood - he'll think he's going to ground after a rabbit,' said Mick.

'Rabbit! Rabbit! Where? Where is it?' whimpered Flash as he tried to run in three directions at once whilst still firmly held by his owner, who was now seriously considering returning Flash to Greyhound Rescue and getting a cat.

Dachdan's owner led him towards the tunnel and indicated that he should walk into it. Dachdan couldn't see the point and tried to walk past it. He was pulled back to the entrance to the flexible plastic pipe and pushed into it by his owner who was beginning to lose patience. Mick then blocked his escape while his owner went to the other end of the tunnel and called him forward, but the curve of the tunnel hid the exit from Dachdan.

Patch had a sudden feeling of blackness and constriction around his ribs which he recognised from the telepathic messages he had received from Dachdan the time he got trapped down a rabbit burrow on the common for a whole night, and thought he was going to die.

Dachdan was now crouched flat in the plastic tunnel and whimpering with panic, giving off waves of fear smell which was unsettling the other dogs.

'Let him out,' Patch barked: 'He's remembering when he was trapped.'

'Patch - help - I can't breathe,' Dachdan was shivering and gasping. His owner was still calling him from the other end of the tunnel, but Dachdan's legs wouldn't work.

Realising that something was wrong, Mick put in

58

an arm and pulled the limp Dachdan out: 'I've never seen that happen before,' he said: 'He doesn't have a heart condition, does he?' Mick was looking worried.

If it will get me out of the rest of this ghastly evening I will happily have a heart condition - whatever that is, Dachdan thought as his owner carried him back to the side of the barn. Once he had put him down, Dachdan began to feel better and his panting slowly returned to normal breathing.

'Poor Dachdan,' Nell nudged him gently with her nose. He began to feel much better.

Mick cast one more worried glance across the barn at Dachdan: 'Is he okay, now?'

'Yes, I think so,' said his owner, running a soothing hand down Dachdan's back.

Mick looked along the line of the remaining dogs thinking he would choose something a little more athletic this time. The evening couldn't get any worse, he thought......he was wrong. Just as he decided to pick Ankle-shredder who had been waiting anxiously for her turn, the barn door, which had been shut after Chico's escape, was pulled noisily back and framed in the entrance was the biggest, blackest dog that Patch had ever seen. Behind it was a skinny human dressed to match in black jeans and a matching 'hoody'. As they moved forwards there was a slight gasp from the assembled humans. Dad whispered to the person next to him: 'Did you ever see the film of The Hound of the Baskervilles?' The lady gave a nervous laugh.

Patch stared at the incomers. There appeared to be something wrong with the human. He had a metal ring through one nostril, two rings through each eyebrow, at least five rings in each ear, a metal stud through his lip and as he spoke, Patch caught the glint of another one through his tongue.

'You train dogs, then?' the human said, realising Mick was in charge.

Mick looked at the huge, male Rottweiller with a sinking heart. The policeman in him was mentally searching the young man for drugs: 'Yes,' he said: 'But...'

'You was a police dog trainer, innit?'

'Yes, but...'

'I want Crusher 'ere trained to catch people and 'old them down, like. You get my meanin'? Like a police dog, innit.' Said the youth, moving his sinister dog forward into the light.

Patch stared at the collar around its thick neck; it glittered with metal embellishments like its owner's face. Then he realised that the dog also had a ring in one ear. The black beast was looking back at him.

'You got a problem wiv somefink, mate?' Its little piggy eyes stared straight at Patch, sending a chill through him which raised the hackles on the back of his neck.

'Er, no...er, mate,' said Patch: 'Er...what's your name?'

'What's yours, then?'

'Er, Pa...Pa...He who sits by the fire and thinks,' said Patch, suddenly deciding his real name may have a more calming effect.

''e calls me Crusher, but my real name, the name my muvver give me, is Daffodil.'

It was a name Patch had heard before, but only in the context of 'Patch - get off the daffodils,' which seemed to coincide with spring and yellow plants.

Mick walked across to the newcomers; there was

something about his walk that suggested 'policeman' to Daffodil, and about the only training he had ever received was that policemen should be attacked to create a diversion while his owner got away. The farmer, Ankle-shredder's owner, was watching the Rottweiller and nervously fingering the mobile phone in his pocket. He understood animals and didn't like the way the dog had suddenly gone very still, or the way its thigh muscles had tensed.

As Mick reached them and said: 'I don't think this class is really suitable for...' Daffodil sprang at him, pulling his unprepared owner over. The farmer took out his phone and dialled 999: 'Police. Dean Manor Farm. Yes. Quick. Rottweiller attacking man.' Then giving Ankle-shredder's lead to Letitia, he and Flash's owner ran across to help Mick who had gone down under the weight of the nine stone Daffodil.

'Crusher! Get off! Get off 'im, innit,' yelled the youth as he struggled to his feet.

As he forced his fangs to meet through Mick's arm, Daffodil vaguely wondered why his owner hadn't run away like he usually did. He also wondered why two unknown humans had joined in to help him attack the policeman, and then why they had lifted his back legs off the ground. Somebody was hitting him with one of the poles from the jumps. As he let go of Mick to turn and bite this person, who was actually Flash's owner, spurred on by imagining Daffodil was Flash, the farmer pushed another of the poles through Daffodil's collar and twisted it, making a choking tourniquet.

'Oy! You're killing 'im, innit. Let 'im go! Crusher, Sit! Innit!'

Daffodil struggled like a mad thing to get at the

farmer but he couldn't breathe, and gradually everything went red and misty and he lost consciousness. The farmer was all for finishing him off but Mick, struggling to his feet with blood pouring from his arm, shouted: 'No! Tie his legs together with some of that string,' he pointed to a roll of orange binder twine at the side of the barn. The farmer cut off some lengths with a pocket knife. Mick pulled a spare lead out of his pocket. To Flash's owner he said: 'You can stop hitting him now and tie this lead round his mouth.' The man reluctantly lowered the pole.

Sirens sounded outside as a police car and dog van came racing down the farm track and Daffodil's owner suddenly seemed to realise he was in deep trouble; he began to back away towards the barn door but his exit was blocked by two large policemen.

Letitia and Dad helped Mick to get his jacket off and roll up his blood-soaked shirt sleeve revealing deep puncture wounds in his arm.

'You must go to hospital,' said Dad. 'I'll take you.'

'We'll take a statement from you later, Mick,' said one of the policemen as he arrested Daffodil's owner for being out of control of a dangerous dog.

'I didn't know 'e was going to do that, innit,' the youth yelled as he was led away: 'Anyway - it's not my dog. I was minding it for a friend, innit.' His voice was cut off as a policeman put a hand on his head and pushed him into the back of the police car.

The dog-handler looked at the prone Daffodil who was now trussed up and immobilised and who had recovered consciousness to discover that he was, apparently, paralysed.

'We'll get this on him,' the dog handler said,

unbuckling the muzzle he was carrying. Helped by the farmer he untied the lead round Daffodil's nose and slipped on the muzzle.

'I know how that feels,' said Flash to Patch as the two men picked the huge black dog up and carried him out to the strongly fortified van.

'He's dead,' said Dachdan.

'No, I saw him move,' said Nell, her voice squeaky with excitement.

'No, I mean he will be dead. He'll be tried and condemned to death. You can't attack humans and get away with it.'

'Wasn't my person brave,' barked Ankle-shredder with excitement: 'If only he had let me help him, my teeth were itching to bite that brute.'

'He'd have swallowed you whole,' said Dachdan.

*

Patch was given a special supper that evening, as were most of the other village dogs as their owners realised how nice their pets really were in comparison with Daffodil. Even Flash's owner began to look at his dog in a slightly different light.

'At least he doesn't kill *people*,' he said to his wife.

'Not yet,' she replied. She preferred cats to dogs but there was no point in getting one, it would have to be replaced too often.

After supper, Patch was in his bed idly listening to his people discussing the evening's excitement, when Nell's thoughts came into his head.

'Oh dear, Patch, are you there? I don't know what to do.'

'What's the problem,' he asked.

'It's my mistress, she's making funny noises and water is running out of her eyes. What can I do? I've

wagged my tail and licked some of the water off her face - very salty it was - but she lifted me up and squeezed me, it was rather uncomfortable.'

Patch sighed. *'You have done as much as you can. I would just go to bed now. It has been a horrible evening for all of us.'*

'I think Ankle-shredder enjoyed it,' said Nell.

'Yes,' said Patch, thinking that if he ever got into a fight, and he sincerely hoped he wouldn't, he would like to have Ankle-shredder on his side.

The telephone rang in the kitchen. Dad picked it up: 'Hello? - Oh, hello, Letitia. Yes...yes...no, don't worry about it...Well, no, it didn't go very well, did it? I don't think agility is really Patch's forté...Well, perhaps it would be a good idea to drop the classes for a while, at least until Mick's arm heals up again...Don't cry, Letitia - it wasn't your fault. Have a strong sherry, dear. It will all look better in the morning...Yes, goodnight, then. Goodnight.'

CHAPTER FIVE

Patch and Dachdan's owners had decided to walk their dogs along the river bank for a change. It was a navigable river with wide paths along each bank where once the narrowboats and loaded barges had been towed along by sturdy horses.

The sun was shining and both dogs were in a good mood, this was normal for Patch but most abnormal for Dachdan, but today his air of permanent gloom had lifted when Patch told him he didn't think there would be any more agility classes.

'What did you think of that Daffodil, then?' Patch asked.

'I thought he probably had the right attitude to agility and especially to that Mick human, but he wasn't a very deep-thinking dog - I mean, if you must attack a human, one of their policemen is not the best choice he could have made. I expect he's dead by now.'

Patch felt the hairs on his neck rise. He had bitten Mick when he had frightened him. He didn't want to be dead. Perhaps he wouldn't mention it. Perhaps it had been forgotten, overshadowed by Daffodil's lethal attack. He jumped as three mallard drakes flew past them down the river and landed splashing and quacking on the water and paddled off into the reeds. He shook himself: 'I can swim,' he said, remembering how he had once rescued Ankle-shredder.

'All dogs can swim,' said Dachdan.

'Do you?' asked Patch.

'Not if I can help it. It's not quite so easy if you are

65

long-bodied, like me. I'm good at swimming in wide circles because it takes me longer to turn.'

'Oh!' said Patch, thinking that if you only swam in circles you would never reach land and would probably, eventually, drown.

Something caught his eye; a flicker of brown fur in the vegetation along the river bank.

'A big mouse!' he said, trotting towards it.

'I am not a mouse,' the water vole said: 'I am a famous endangered species. Hurt me and you will be in deep trouble with humans. I'm protected.'

'I see no protection,' said Dachdan, trotting up.

'Dachdan! Patch! LEAVE! Come here, NOW!' said their owners, together.

'See what I mean?' said the water vole, sliding his furry body into the water and disappearing into a hole in the river bank.

The two dogs had obediently turned back towards their owners but they, having been obeyed were continuing their conversation and once more ignoring the dogs.

'I thought they wanted us to come,' said Dachdan.

'Probably something to do with that mouse-thing, what did it say it was?' Patch asked.

'A famous endangered species. That's not a name. Looked more like a rat to me.'

In the distance behind them they could hear the noise of an engine. The sound grew gradually louder, chug, chug, chug, chug, and as Patch turned to look, slightly apprehensive in case they were in danger of being run over, a brightly painted narrowboat came slowly round the bend in the river.

'It's a swimming house,' said Patch.

'Odd sort of house, it's got the garden on the roof,'

said Dachdan looking at the mass of potted plants which nearly covered the boat.

'It's not a house...it's a kennel. Look, there's the dog at the back,' said Patch: 'Woof,' he barked with surprise.

'And woof to you,' said the dog, putting it's paws up on the edge of the boat as it caught sight of them.

'There's a human with it,' said Dachdan.

The man driving the narrowboat slowed down to walking pace and began to chat to the dogs' owners.

'Where are you going?' Dachdan asked the dog.

'No idea, mate. We do this every summer, week after week, river after river, canal after canal, but we always seem to end up at home again.'

'Don't you mind being away all the time? Don't you ever go for walks?' asked Patch.

'All the time, mate. There are these wide paths all along the way. I get off several times a day.'

This life sounded idyllic to Patch.

'Are you Australian?' asked Dachdan: 'I knew an Australian Heeler once who said 'mate' all the time.'

'No, mate, I'm from London, well originally London. There were some other humans; I lived with them, but they didn't like me and I got tired of being hit. I never knew what I had done wrong, so I ran away. Then, just when I had worked out the warmest places to sleep and the best litter bins to eat at, somebody put a lead on me, shoved me in a van and took me to a very noisy prison under some railway arches. Battersea Dogs Home they called it: the place was full of barking, coughing dogs. I really hated it and I felt ill. Then these people came and rescued me and took me to their boat. Look out! I'm coming down.'

67

The boat had pulled in close enough to the bank for the dog to leap ashore.

'The name's Brindley,' he said. The three dogs walked, stiff-legged around each other as they got to know each others' scent: 'He was a famous canal builder, I'm told. My people are mad on canals and these narrowboats.'

The water vole stuck his head out of the water, saw the dogs, said: 'Oh no! They are multiplying,' and disappeared back under the bank.

'What breed are you?' Dachdan asked, peering up at Brindley who was a bit taller than the other two.

'Collie cross, they tell me. My mother was a collie but I don't remember her ever saying what my father was. I probably inherited my coat from him.' He shook himself and the shining auburn hair lifted and settled around him again; he was a very handsome dog, Patch thought, rather glad that Ankle-shredder wasn't with them; she might be rather too easily attracted by shining brown eyes and long legs.

A whistle from the boat took Brindley's attention and as it pulled in to the bank he leapt on board again and turned round: 'Do you want to come up?' he said.

Patch moved to the edge of the bank and looked at the narrowboat which was already beginning to pull away: 'I don't think I ...' he said, as the bank collapsed under his front feet where it had been undermined by the current. As he slid into the water he felt a sharp pain in his front paw. He swam in a small circle and pulled himself back out of the water, then lay down to inspect his stinging paw: 'It's bleeding,' he said: 'Something bit me!'

'Of course I bit you. You have wrecked the

entrance to my dwelling and allowed ingress to the water. My burrow is now flooded,' said the water vole angrily: 'What's the good of being a protected endangered species when this sort of vandalism is permitted to occur?'

'What's vandalism?' Patch asked Dachdan.

'What you just did to his front door,' said Dachdan, his day was getting better all the time: 'Wait till I tell Ankle-shredder you fell in the river and got bitten by a mouse.'

'How many times do I have to tell you I am not a mouse...Oh forget it! I have to go and find a new residence now. I don't think much of the protection I'm getting. Never a conservationist around when you need one.' He looked back over his shoulder at Dachdan as he swam away: '...and I am a water vole...goodness knows what you are. Nature seems to have treated you with some hostility.'

'Come up here and say that,' Dachdan barked, but the water vole dived and disappeared.

'You'll probably get some horrible disease from that bite,' said Dachdan, cheerfully.

'Some friend you are,' said Patch, limping off after his person who had missed all the fun and was just disappearing around the bend ahead.

'Patch, you stupid dog; you've been swimming...not like you. You'll have to stay outside till you dry off when we get home.'

'He fell in,' said Dachdan.

'Shut-up!' said Patch, shaking himself and spraying water into Dachdan's eyes.

The two dogs and their owners strolled on beside the slow flowing river. A moorhen called from the reeds which rustled in the gentle breeze and the sun shone warm on Patch's back, raising steam from his rapidly drying coat. This is a good place, he thought. He had just turned to share this thought with Dachdan when a movement up ahead took his attention; a human and a large dog were coming towards them...a large BLACK dog. In an instant Patch recognised them: 'It's Mick...and Daffodil.'

'It can't be...he's dead.'

'He's not dead. He's with Mick and they are coming towards us. Quick run!'

'Where?' said Dachdan, worriedly watching Patch who seemed to be trying to run in two directions at once.

A cloud drifted across the sun and there was a sudden chill to the wind. The moorhen stopped calling and a sinister silence seemed to precede Daffodil's progress along the river bank.

'Run where?' asked Dachdan again, looking at all the open space around them.

'There, quick, down the bank. It's shallow there and there is a little beach with an overhang. We can hide under there until they have gone past.' The two dogs crept silently down the bank keeping low to the ground with their tails firmly tucked into their hindquarters.

'Oh no! Not you again...it's like being haunted,' said the water vole.

'Shhh! It's Daffodil,' said Patch.

'Can't be. Daffodils are spring flowers. This is the wrong time of year,' said the water vole: 'What is it you find so frightening about a mere botanical species?'

'Be quiet, rat! We are not after you. Don't draw attention to us here or we will be,' Dachdan snarled.

'You can go after it if you want. I'm not...it bites,' said Patch looking at his paw: 'Daffodil is a very dangerous dog,' he explained to the water vole.

'Oh. You are obviously terrified. For me the devil incarnate is the mink. If you two promise to harass any mink you may encounter, I will permit you to tarry on my private beach until your fear of the current danger has ameliorated.'

'I can't understand half of what this mouse thing says,' said Patch, staring at the water vole.

'Where did you learn all those long words?' asked Dachdan, who was secretly impressed and busily storing new words in his mind, intent on impressing Ankle-shredder next time they met. If they ever did meet again, he thought, remembering Daffodil was approaching on the towpath above them.

'I grew up on a river in Oxford,' said the water vole. This explanation meant nothing to the two dogs but they didn't like to say so.

There was a sudden flurry and snuffling above them and Daffodil and half the bank came down on top of them: 'Hello you two...I thought it was you,' said the black monster.

There was a muffled squeak followed by a shout from behind the earth fall which had covered the entrance to the water vole's new burrow: 'That's it - I've had enough. I'm going back to Oxford, if I survive this entombment.'

'What was that?' said Daffodil, looking round.

'A sort of mouse thing, water...something,' said Patch, glad to have Daffodil's attention diverted.

'For the very last time,' came the muffled voice: 'I am a water vole...if that is too difficult to remember try Arvicola Terrestris. Goodbye...Oxford here I

71

come.'

'Where is this Oxford, then?' asked Patch, beginning to relax as Daffodil hadn't eaten either of them yet.

'Many miles away,' said the water vole: 'Though the distance will present me with no problem. I have a penchant for navigation. I shall return to where I can listen to the wind in the willows.'

Daffodil pinpointed the sound in the bank and began to scrabble at the loose soil he had dislodged.

'Max! Come here!' Mick's voice sent a shiver through Dachdan and Patch.

'My new name,' explained Daffodil as he crashed obediently up the bank onto the path.

'Well, if that was a dead Daffodil I don't wish to meet a live one,' said Patch.

'That Mick must have taken him on to train him to behave. I thought this was going to be a quiet walk,' said Dachdan: 'What did the rat say it's other name was?'

'Harvey something. Come on, we might as well get back onto the path again.' Patch scrambled up the bank, dislodging more soil onto the beach.

'Vandals!' the mud-muffled shout followed them along the path.

Dad and Dachdan's owner were standing further along the towpath with Mick who was demonstrating some of the training he had done with Daffodil. The sun had come out again and was bouncing off Daffodil's gleaming black coat as he sat like a statue beside Mick, looking at him and waiting for the next command: 'Down!' said Mick. Daffodil dropped flat: 'Sit!'. He sat up: 'Stand!' He stood: 'Round!' He moved behind Mick and sat on his other side.

'He's been brainwashed,' said Dachdan.

'Which can only be a good thing,' said Patch, wondering how much luck Mick would have with Flash, or even Dachdan, he thought, looking at his companion.

'Why are you staring at me?' asked Dachdan, his voice growling with aggression as his mind caught the tail end of Patch's unflattering thought: 'Don't compare me with that no-brain greyhound.'

Daffodil heard Dachdan's growl, picked up on his aggression and was instantly triggered into an action from his former life. He sprang towards them in attack mode, hair bristling on his spine. Dachdan shrieked, spun round and went haring off along the towpath, his ears flying out behind him.

Mick stopped Daffodil with one very fierce command and gave him a biscuit for returning to him. Dachdan, by then, was just a small terrified shape disappearing round a bend in the distance with his owner in pursuit. Patch wondered whether he should follow Dachdan and tell him that Daffodil was now on a lead. He sent him a telepathic message to this effect, but Dachdan's brain was so full of the fear that he was about to be eaten, he didn't pick it up.

Mick was trying to apologise to Dad, but he was so impressed with Mick's recall training, he brushed the apology aside: 'I'm going to try that with Patch,' he said.

'I'll do it for chicken,' said Patch, but nobody except Daffodil heard him.

'Heel!' said Mick, turning back the way they had come. Daffodil looked over his shoulder as he walked away and said: 'Tell that weird-looking friend of yours to control his aggression before it gets him into trouble.'

This remark left Patch speechless as he watched the muscled black bottom receding along the path beside Mick. He wondered how Daffodil had lost his tail and who had been brave enough to bite it off. Could only have been a bigger, more aggressive Rottweiller, he thought, shivering slightly at the thought of something larger and more dangerous than Daffodil.

'Come on, Patch...er I mean, Heel! Patch,' said Dad, turning back after the disappearing figure of Dachdan's owner who was now running after his dog.

'Where's me biscuit, then?' asked Patch, but Dad didn't seem to have taken in that part of the training.

'Dachdan, it's all right, he's gone...on a lead.' beamed Patch. All he got in return from Dachdan's fear crazed mind was a sort of senseless gibbering.

Dachdan was now about a quarter of a mile away and galloping up the steeply sloping path beside the bridge. This path led straight onto the road into the village. He was going home...or so he thought.

'There it is!' said the dog warden to Anna, his young trainee assistant. He had parked his van just past the bridge and walked back to scan the river bank on both sides of the road. They had been told to look out for a lost dog about Dachdan's size which was missing from Groffholm, a village two miles away: 'It's coming up the slope. Get the net.'

As Dachdan, now severely out of breath, struggled up the last few feet of the slope at the end of the bridge parapet, the net, fixed to a long pole, was expertly dropped over him: 'Got him!' said the dog warden.

He grabbed Dachdan by the scruff of his neck, untangled him from the net and carried the now completely shocked dog to the van where he was placed in a cage. Initially he felt safe. Daffodil would not be able to get through the strong metal mesh which now surrounded him. Before he could check how close Daffodil was, the van doors were closed. The engine started and the van moved off. In a few minutes he would be home and safe.

'Good boy, Gregory,' said Anna, turning round in her seat.

Dachdan began to calm down, though he was still panting hard, then he began to worry again. They should have been home by now but they were still driving along narrow country lanes.

'Soon be home, Gregory,' said the girl in her nice soothing voice.

Who's Gregory? Dachdan wondered, knowing there was no point in trying to reach the minds of these humans with his question: '*Patch, where are you?*' he beamed.

'*Still by the river. We're coming back. Has your person caught up with you? Don't worry, Daffodil's gone.*'

'*I don't know where my person is. I'm in a van. I don't know where I am. I was caught in a trap on the bridge.*'

None of this made any sense to Patch.

'*They keep calling me Gregory. I think it is a case of mistaken identity.*'

'*Unlikely...there can't be anyone else as ug...unusual as you,*' said Patch.

'*Hang on, I think we are slowing down,*' said

Dachdan.

The van turned into a gravelled drive and crunched to a stop in front of a large house. A lady who was working in the garden put down her trowel and came across to the van.

'Have you found him?' she asked.

'Yes. He was by the river, about two miles away near the bridge.'

'How did he get that far?' she said.

The dog warden opened the back doors of the van: 'You're home, Gregory,' he said.

'Oh!' said the lady, sounding disappointed: 'That's not Gregory. Gregory is a Sealyham and handsome. Goodness knows what that is. Oh dear!'

'Really! Who's this little chap then?' said the dog warden: 'He's not wearing a collar. Just a minute.' He went round to the front of the van, and came back with a small machine which he passed over the back of Dachdan's neck as Anna held him. Dachdan ducked but it didn't hurt: 'No - he's not been micro-chipped.' He closed the back doors of the van as he said: 'Well, I'm very sorry, Mrs Collins. We'll keep looking for Gregory.'

He started the engine and said: 'We'd better go back to the bridge where we picked this one up in case his owner's looking for him. Somebody must love him, the ugly little blighter looks well cared for.'

'Just you wait till dogs take over the world,' Dachdan beamed at him: *'I'll make you sorry for that unkind remark... 'baldy',* he finished, glaring at the back of the shiny pink head in front of him. It looked like a serious case of mange to Dachdan and he moved to the back of the cage to avoid the possibility

of catching it. He aimed his thoughts at Patch: *'Where are you?'*

'Still waiting below the bridge. You're person has gone to see if you've gone home. Dad is still looking for you here.'

'Keep him there. We are on our way back.'

Dad muttered something that sounded like 'damn dog's run home, I'll bet.' He tugged on the lead: 'Come on, Patch'

'No. He's coming.'

'Patch - I said 'come on'. Heel! Good boy.' 'You're not supposed to say 'Good boy' if I don't obey you,' said Patch, leaning back on his lead and digging his feet into the soft earth of the river bank, seeing flaws in Dad's dog training skills and thinking that he himself would make a much better dog trainer …perhaps he could practise on Nell. His feet began to slip so he sat down.

'Get up, Patch - what's the matter with you?' The tug on his collar which accompanied this order was quite painful.

'Do you realise how much I am suffering for you?' he beamed at Dachdan, as he lay down to get even more purchase on the ground.

'It's me that is suffering. I'm the one being kidnapped…or should that be dognapped?'

'Get up, Patch!' Dad pushed his foot under Patch's stomach and tried to lift him with his toe as he pulled the front end up.

'That really hurt!' Patch yelped.

'What's the matter with your dog?' It was the dog warden, who had stopped his van on the bridge and was looking at them over the parapet: 'There is no need to kick it, sir.'

Dachdan had heard Patch yelp and began to bark. Patch barked back and tried to pull Dad towards the van.

'I wasn't kicking him. He wouldn't get up, but he seems all right now. What's that barking in your van…it sounds familiar and my dog seems to recognise it.'

'Have you lost a dog, sir?'

'Yes, well my friend has.'

'Can you describe the lost dog.'

'Careful!' beamed Dachdan at Dad, who of course, didn't get the message.

'Well, not pretty…sort of dachshund body with an ugly head which looks too big for the body.'

'That's another one to sort out come world dog-domination,' muttered Dachdan, through snarly teeth.

The story all came out and the dog warden lent Dad a lead to take Dachdan home. As he lifted him out of the van, Dachdan looked nervously round him: 'Has Daffodil gone?' he asked.

'Yes, hours ago. But if we ever meet him again I reckon you had better practice being a subservient underdog.'

'Subservience is not in my nature…but maybe I could fake it for Daffodil,' Dachdan sighed: 'Patch, I'm stressed out. I just want to get home and sleep.' The two dogs walked quietly up the road, side by side behind Dad as he took out his mobile phone and called Dachdan's owner.

CHAPTER SIX

Patch was sitting in the sunshine outside the village shop, the end of his lead tied to a ring in the wall, while Dad was inside the shop talking to some other villagers. He was quite happy to sit there by himself because it gave him time to think; when there were other dogs around he became easily distracted. He was just getting deeply into wondering why humans controlled dogs, when really dogs were so much more intelligent, and trying to catch the stray thought that had crossed his mind on the Agility evening, that maybe it was really the other way round and dogs controlled humans to make sure that they had a warm bed and a constant supply of food; when something white caught his eye.

A rather hairy white terrier of almost his own size and build was just cresting the brow of the hill into the village. The dog appeared to be alone, no human followed behind. This might not have been so unusual on the common but dogs didn't normally walk alone on the roads in the traffic...not that there was any at the moment.

It trotted on towards the village green, saw Patch and slowing to a walk, came towards him, warily poised between greeting and battle depending on Patch's reaction to him. Patch stayed sitting down in a very unthreatening manner. Then stood up for a bit of mutual sniffing.

'You're new here. Who are you?' asked Patch, having established that he was not going to have to put up a show of aggression to defend himself.

'My people call me Gregory. My mother called me Traveller. She said, 'You will go far,' and I have.

79

Yesterday I got a lift in a car and went to Brighton. Turned out to be the wrong way but it was a very comfortable car, and they had biscuits.'

'You're lost,' said Patch: 'The dog warden was looking for you.'

'What does lost mean, boy?'

'You…er, don't know where you live.'

'Of course I know where I live. It's over there,' Gregory turned in the direction of Groffholm: 'I can navigate my way back by the sun, the scent of the woods and the soil texture…if I want to…which I don't. I'm on a quest, you see. I'm trying to return to Wales, to the land of my fathers.'

Patch was puzzled by the plural: 'How many fathers do you have, then?' His scant knowledge of reproduction suddenly called into question.

'No, no boy, it's an expression, means my homeland, where my roots, my ancestors, were. I'm a Sealyham you see…a Sealyham terrier.'

This was a new breed to Patch. At that moment Flash's owner led his dog out of their garden gate and across the green, heading for the common. Gregory let out a series of the highest pitched barks Patch had ever heard. Even higher than Chico's. He winced.

'Oh, sorry, boy. I've got this very high pitched bark, something not quite right with my vocal cords. Down the vets they call me the Helium Sealyham…don't know why, must be the bark though…until I barked there they used to call me Gregory.'

'Perhaps you shouldn't bark too often,' said Patch, shaking his head to try to get the ringing out of his ears.

'Patch, who is that?' beamed Flash, but he didn't wait for a reply because he had seen a squirrel racing up the chestnut tree on the corner of the green. Patch didn't bother to answer as he watched Flash trying to climb the tree.

'Someone should tell him dogs don't climb trees,' said Gregory.

'Oh, all he thinks about is killing things. He nearly killed Chico once.'

'Who's Chico?'

'A very small and irritating dog - lives in the village. Barks a bit like you.'

'You find me irritating?' Gregory grew an inch or so and his eyes grew larger.

'No, no,' said Patch, quickly: 'I find you most interesting. How do you manage to get these humans to take you on your ...er quest in their cars?'

Out of the corner of his eye he saw Flash's owner strangling his dog away from the chestnut tree, then dragging him off up the road.

'Well, if you listen, boy, I'll tell you.'

Patch gave Gregory his full attention.

'Right, well what I do is I go to the end of my drive and stand in the road waiting for a stranger to drive by. I put on this lost expression, see.' He demonstrated, tucking his tail firmly into his hindquarters and adopting a worried expression, constantly moving his head around as if searching for his owner.

A car pulled up outside the shop.

'Help!' called Dachdan from inside: 'He's taking me to the vet for an injection.'

Dachdan's owner got out and came over to them: 'Hello, little fellow,' he said, approaching Gregory:

81

'Are you lost?'

'No. And you're no good to me. I'm going to Wales, not the vet. I'm off. Goodbye, boy,' he said to Patch as he dodged the human hand which was reaching down to see if there was an identity tag on his collar.

'Good luck. Hope you get to your father…fathers.'

Gregory trotted off across the green in a north-westerly direction. His lost look had changed to the purposeful one of a dog who knew exactly where he was going.

'Keep in touch,' Patch beamed.

'Nice to meet you, boy.'

'Who's that?' Dachdan asked.

'That, is Gregory.'

'What! *The* Gregory?'

'Apparently.'

'How on earth could they have mistaken me for him?…He's white!'

'And he barks like Chico…only worse.'

'Well! Makes you despair of the human race doesn't it.'

'Probably,' said Patch, trying to pick up the threads of his previous thoughts about human versus dog intelligence.

'Is he going to live here?' Dachdan asked.

'No. He's on a quest. Wants to go to Wales and find his father…or fathers…it's a bit confusing.'

'He's lost. Someone should tell the dog warden,' said Dachdan.

'He's not lost,' Patch answered, feeling a twinge of envy at Gregory's capable and positive outlook on life. Gregory, he thought, was a born leader. He took no instruction from humans.

Dachdan's owner gave up trying to catch up with Gregory who was now trotting fast in the direction of Wales, and returned to the car.

'Can't anyone save me,' Dachdan wailed as the car engine started.

'Sorry, I'm tied up,' said Patch.

'You don't care,' said Dachdan.

This was correct, but Patch didn't say so. He watched the car carry Dachdan away towards the vet's, then sat down again and tried to count the ways in which his superior intelligence manipulated his human family pack to his advantage.

Food…well, granted, they did feed him, but no matter how hard he beamed them the message, it wasn't often on chicken.

He tried something else. Walks…sometimes, if he sat in the kitchen staring at his lead hanging on the back of the door a passing human might notice and, possibly, take him out. Again, not really successful. This was beginning to depress him. They should really allow him to snooze in that sunny patch on the sofa. Nell said Madame Letitia let her do this at her house but the one time Patch had tried it, Mum had dumped him on the floor with a degrading tap on his behind.

Now thoroughly depressed, he realised he was never going to be pack leader in his human pack. He gazed across the green in the direction Gregory had taken…Gregory, gloriously free, in charge of his life and on a quest. Patch beamed a message after him: *'If I can get away, would you like some company on your quest?'*

'Of course, boy. It's always better to travel as a pack, you'd be welcome. As welcome as a welcome in

the hillside.'

Patch had a momentary qualm as he wondered whether Gregory was really quite sane; he did say some very strange things. Then he decided it was time for some positive thinking - and action. He stood up and shook himself, feeling his collar rattle against his neck - good - it was still loose. He leaned back on it and as it slipped up behind his ears, he twisted his head slightly.

'Easy,' he grunted as the empty collar dropped to the ground at the end of the lead which was still tied to the ring in the shop wall.

'Wait for me,' he beamed at Gregory as he picked up his scent and began to follow it across the green.

'Ouch! Sadist!' The shriek came into his mind and startled him for a second until he realised it was Dachdan at the vet's. He didn't have time for him now, he had to catch up with Gregory.

Nobody saw Patch cross the green and enter the wood. Gregory's scent didn't follow the path, but disappeared into the bushes. The trees and heavy vegetation dimmed the light from the sun and Patch felt a tiny frisson of fear as he remembered he had once come face to face with a Big Cat in these same woods. He sniffed the air, then beamed a message at Gregory: *'Can you smell cat, at all?'*

'No, boy, and there's no time for cat-chasing. Quests is serious business. Hurry and catch up, I've slowed down for you.'

Patch couldn't smell cat, either, and he forced his short legs into a gallop. As the wind caught his ears his spirits lifted - he was free and in charge of his own life. Nobody would tell him what to do now.

'Hurry up, boy!' Except Gregory, of course. This

thought slightly took the edge off his excitement but he pushed it away.

The scent of Gregory was getting stronger and as he forced his way through the undergrowth he saw him in a clearing, showing up white against the dark green of the rhododendrons. Patch was out of breath and panting hard as he reached him.

'Not very fit are you, boy.' Gregory said.

'Well, it would be easier if we could stick to the paths,' Patch panted.

'Paths is for wimps. We are making a bee-line for Wales.'

Patch couldn't see what bees had got to do with anything but he didn't say so. He hoped that as they came to know each other better, some of Gregory's more obscure remarks would become clearer.

'Come on, then.' Gregory set off again at a brisk trot and Patch followed, ducking as branches which Gregory had pushed aside, sprang back in his face. He slowed slightly and let the gap between them increase.

After a quarter of an hour they came to the edge of the wood and were faced with a field full of cows. Patch realised that they were on Ankle-shredder's farm. He wasn't keen on cows and moved to go round the edge of the field.

'What are you doing, boy? It's this way - bee-line remember?' said Gregory, heading straight for the cows.

Patch still hung back: 'Do you know about cows?' he asked.

'Haven't had much to do with them.' Gregory trotted on. The cows lifted their heads and began to walk towards him.

'They sometimes chase dogs,' said Patch, as the cows tossed their heads and broke into a lumbering trot. Gregory slowed down.

'Why?' he asked.

'I don't know, perhaps they are getting their own back for the times Ankle-shredder has nipped their heels - she's a Lancashire Heeler, you know.'

'I don't know what you're talking about, boy, but I think I'll come along the fence with you, they're quite large, aren't they.'

'HEY! What are you doing, upsetting my cows? Only I am allowed to do that.' It was Ankle-shredder, racing across the field towards them.

'Dieu! Look at that, boy. Oh, she's gorgeous! D'you think she'd like to come to Wales with us?'

'Hello, Patch. Who's this?' said Ankle-shredder, sinking her sharp teeth into Gregory's rump.

'Ouch!' he said: 'Fiery as well. What a bitch!'

'This is Gregory,' said Patch, trying to push himself between the starry-eyed Sealyham and Ankle-shredder who was looking particularly beautiful. He growled at Gregory: 'She's my friend. I'll ask her if she wants to come with us. Annie, would you like to join Gregory's...I mean our quest?'

'What's a quest? Is it like a pack? I could only join a pack if I was made the leader, or at least alpha bitch.'

'It's like a journey - we're going back to find the land of Gregory's fathers.'

'How many does he have, then?'

'Don't go there - we're going to a place called Wales.'

'Where the fish are?'

'What fish?'

'Whales aren't fish, they're mammals,' said Gregory: 'Those cows are getting a bit close again.'

Ankle-shredder trotted towards them barking, and they thought better of it and returned to grazing.

'Strong personality - lovely voice,' said Gregory.

Patch remembered the awful scream which passed for a bark when Gregory got excited and hoped he wouldn't do it too often on the way to Wales.

'You coming, then?' Gregory asked Ankle-shredder.

'Will it take long? Only we've got milking in half an hour and I have to see the cows into the milking parlour and then turn them out again afterwards. My job is very important, you know. I'm a working dog. What are you for?'

'For? What do you mean?' asked Gregory, puzzled.

'He's a Sealyham,' said Patch, also wondering what Sealyhams did. He was quite relieved that he was a crossbreed and wasn't committed to any special line of work like pedigree dogs. He sniffed: 'Can you smell cat, Annie?'

'Yes. It's over there,' she said, looking towards the wood.

Patch's knees went weak.

'It's old Tom - one of the farm cats.' She was still waiting for an answer from the Sealyham.

Patch moved away and sniffed around the base of one of the fence posts, then concentrated on scent-marking it while he composed himself. He remembered that his father was a Bull Terrier and searched within himself for the strong, brave genes that must be there, and felt a bit silly as he watched the old, moth-eaten, lame black cat limp back towards the farm yard.

'Are there many more woods on the way to Wales?' he asked Gregory.

'I expect so - forests as well and when we get there, mountains and wild places. Oh! it will be wonderful.'

'So what *do* Sealyhams do?' Ankle-shredder asked again.

'Oh, we're for digging out foxes and badgers but there's not much call for it any more. Times have changed since my ancestors were bred for the job.'

'Why would you want to dig out foxes and badgers - they bite,' said Ankle-shredder.

'That's probably why they stopped,' said Patch.

'Are you suggesting we are a cowardly race, boy?'

'No! No.' Patch backed away, thinking fast: 'Anybody who could set out on a quest of...how many miles is it?...can't be cowardly.'

'Time to go. Work to do.' Ankle-shredder trotted off after the old black cat.

Gregory hadn't answered Patch's question. Patch hoped it wasn't far because he had experienced a sudden pang of loneliness as he watched Annie disappear. He had never felt lonely before and couldn't quite work out what the strange sensation was, but it wasn't pleasant.

'Shame, that,' said Gregory, also looking after Ankle-shredder: 'It would have been nice to have her accompany us on my quest. We'd better get on.' He turned away and headed for the wood which folded itself round the other side of the cows' field.

Patch thought he could hear Dad whistling for him. He stopped and turned towards the sound, years of obedience controlling his movements.

'Are you coming?' Gregory called: 'Come on,

you're not giving up already are you - didn't take you for a wimp.'

Patch sighed and trotted after Gregory. Maybe Wales wasn't far, he hoped they would be back by the evening because that was when he was fed and he was feeling a bit hungry. He'd already had quite a long walk on the common before Dad had tied him up outside the shop and he always got some biscuits when they got back from their walk.

They continued, mostly in silence for the next half hour, finally leaving the wood and crossing fields that took them on a steady climb up a hill. Reaching the top they both stopped to catch their breath as they looked down across the valley and a river to much higher hills on the other side.

'Are we nearly there? Are those the mountains?' Patch asked. They looked a long way away.

'I don't think so, the mountains in my memory are far higher than that. Come on.'

Going down the hill was much easier and it wasn't long before they reached the river: 'Right! Now we need a bridge,' said Gregory: 'This is going to interfere with my bee-line.'

'I can swim,' said Patch, looking doubtfully at the swiftly flowing water and comparing it with the calm surface of the old gravel pit lake he had rescued Ankle-shredder from, some time ago.

'Can you?' Gregory didn't seem keen to try.

'I'll just test it for water speed,' said Patch, moving down the bank, feeling rather proud of himself for taking the initiative. It was slippery and he slid the last twenty centimetres to the waters edge, dislodging a small chunk of earth and grass.

'I don't believe it!' The outraged squeak came from

right beside him: 'You again! Have you nothing better to do than persecute me…it's no wonder I'm an endangered species. How many of us have you destroyed by drowning and heart failure, not to mention suffocation due to tunnel collapse.'

'What's that squeaking?' Gregory called from the top of the bank.

'It's Harvey something,' said Patch as three centimetres or so of busy water swirled around his toes. It felt rather chilly.

'Arvicola Terrestris! The least you can do is get my name right after destroying three of my homes,' squeaked the water vole, hysterically.

'I'm sorry,' said Patch: 'I just wanted to see how fast the water was going.'

'Well why don't you test it properly and jump in,' said the water vole, nastily. His expression convinced Patch that throwing himself into the fast-moving river would probably not be one of his better ideas.

'Is this Oxford, then?' he asked the water vole as he backed away from the waters edge.

'Careful! Now you've kicked half my bed into the river. No, of course this isn't Oxford. Oxford is miles away. It will take me about a year to get there, and henceforth I will build my homes on the other side of the river as a dog-avoidance exercise.'

A year! Patch had difficulty imagining a whole year of travelling. He looked after the tiny bundle of hay floating down the river and was overcome with a sudden strong longing for his own cosy bed: 'I'm sorry about your bed,' he said: 'We're going to Wales. Do you know how far it is?'

'No idea, and if I did know I wouldn't tell you, but if it is in the same direction as Oxford I might change my plans and head for the sea. I can't cope with the constant stress of worrying that any minute you will appear again to bring another dwelling crashing down around my ears.'

Patch thought this a little unfair, after all it was Daffodil who had destroyed the last one.

'That's a rat you've got there, boy,' said Gregory, leaning over the edge of the bank: 'Quick, kill it and we'll have it for supper.'

'It's not a rat it's, OUCH!' Patch leapt backwards as the water vole sank sharp teeth into his front paw.

'Attack is the best form of defence,' squeaked the water vole as it dived into the river, narrowly avoiding Patch as he lost his footing and slipped into the water; the current took him and he was swept into the middle of the fast-flowing river where he began to paddle madly to stay afloat.

'What are you doing, boy? I thought we were going to look for a bridge,' yelled Gregory: 'Hey! Come back, that's not the way to Wales.'

Patch suddenly didn't care about Wales or quests or Gregory, but found that he cared a lot about not drowning. He could still hear Gregory who was trying to follow him along the bank but was getting left behind. He swallowed a mouthful of water and coughed and began to panic. Then after what seemed a lifetime of terror, the rushing water slammed him against a fallen tree. As he scrabbled frantically at the branches and the cold water tugged at his back end, trying to drag him onwards, Patch had visions of being carried miles away. Harvey…thing had said it was this way to the sea. He didn't like the sea-side; he'd been there once and the pebbles had hurt his feet; though, come to think of it, he wouldn't mind some pebbles under his feet at the moment. Finally a swirling wave lifted him high enough to climb onto the trunk of the old alder tree which had fallen into the river the night before. He clung there shivering.

'There you are, boy! You are a fast swimmer, I could hardly keep up. I'm impressed.'

Patch didn't answer. His body and mind were one cold, shivering mass.

'Come on, boy! Come back here. I've found a way we can get across in the dry - there's a bridge up ahead.'

'Though it seems to have escaped your notice, I *am* across...when I get the strength to face balancing along this tree trunk,' said Patch.

'Oh! yes - well, I'll just go round by the bridge and join you. You didn't manage to get the rat, did you? I could do with a snack after all that running.'

Patch took a deep breath and began to get his quivering body under control. A spider thought about attaching one corner of its web to his nose, then changed its mind when he sneezed. He watched Gregory climb the slope to the road over the bridge, and disappear behind the parapet as he began to cross. A white van slowed on its approach, then stopped on the bridge.

'Oh! no. Not him again!' the dog warden said to himself, pulling on the hand-brake and opening the door.

Patch continued to watch the end of the parapet, waiting for Gregory to re-appear on his side of the river. The van drove away.

'You still there, Patch?' The question arrived in his mind.

'Where else? I'm nearly warm enough to move

onto the bank when you get here.'

'Well, it's like this, you see. There might be a bit of a delay before I can rejoin you. I have a slight problem.'

'Problem?'

'Yes. I've been...er...dognapped.'

'You've what? This is no time for a nap.'

'No, no. Dognapped. It's with being so well known, you know, well, famous, even. I was recognised on the bridge and now I suspect I am being taken home. A real nuisance, we were doing so well before you stopped to talk to the rat.'

'You cannot blame me. It was the river that stopped us. Who's taking you home? Was it the human who stopped on the bridge? What about me?'

'That was no human. That was my enemy. The dog warden. First chance I get I'll bite him. I'll try to rejoin you sometime tomorrow, then we can continue the quest.'

'You could have tried to lead him to me here. I don't mind being dognapped. I want to go home. I'm cold and I want my supper.'

'You should have caught the rat. Don't despair, boy. I'll join you tomorrow.'

Yes. After you've had some supper and a warm night's sleep, Patch thought. Why did he ever think joining Gregory on his quest was a good idea? He began to shiver again. The sun was low in the sky now and a chattering flock of jackdaws soared and tumbled above him, playing with the wind as they made their way towards their roost for the night. He couldn't lie here all night, he had to reach dry land. Something moved in the water below him.

'There's a novelty. I didn't realise dogs roosted in

trees at night. I suppose you'll be destroying birds nests next,' said the water vole.

'I'm stuck. This is your fault. You didn't have to bite me again, I wasn't going to hurt you.'

'Can't be too careful. I have innumerable enemies.' He swam away upstream leaving a small v-shaped wake behind him.

That is one rude rat, thought Patch. This short exchange with the belligerent water vole had made him angry. He didn't often get angry but the unusual emotion now gave him the energy surge he needed to get moving. If he fell in again he would swim to shore, if one small rat could do it then so could he.

In spite of a couple of slips which raised the hairs on the back of his neck, he managed to scramble along the trunk and through the branches to the roots of the tree and, climbing over them, he jumped down onto the ground, scratched and bruised but feeling pretty good. He shook himself hard and long, spraying water out of his soaked coat in all directions. An owl hooted in the wood on the other side of the river...somewhere over there were his warm bed and his supper. His stomach rumbled. He started off towards the bridge hoping that maybe the dog warden would come back and take him home as well.

As he trotted along the towpath, his mind fixed on his supper, his concentration on food was interrupted. 'Hey!' The single sharp bark came from behind him. He turned as the dog bounded towards him through the gathering dusk.

'Nice to meet you, again.' The dog circled him, tail wagging, and Patch suddenly remembered him. This was Brindley, the dog from the floating house on the river: 'You been swimming, then? The river's running a bit too fast for safe swimming,' said Brindley.

'I found that out,' said Patch, unwilling to admit that it was a nip from a water vole which had tipped him into the water.

A woman came round the bend and saw the two dogs together. She called Brindley and looked round for Patch's owner, surprised to find anyone on this lonely stretch of the river at this time of day.

'Where's your human?' asked Brindley.

'At home. I'm a bit lost. It's a long story,' said Patch.

Catching them up, the woman bent down to look for a collar on Patch, then realised he was soaking wet: 'I reckon you've fallen in the river, little lad. We'd better take you back and dry you out, then find out where you came from.' She made a loop of the lead she was carrying and dropped it over Patch's head.

They made their way back along the towpath until Patch could see Brindley's floating house. There was a curl of smoke drifting from its chimney. Brindley trotted over the plank which led from the bank onto the deck of the narrowboat.

'Is it safe?' Patch asked, not wishing to find himself back in dangerous, vole-infested waters.

'Course it is. The boat's tied to the bank for the night, we're not going anywhere.'

They stepped down into a small open area, then entered the cabin through narrow double doors. Patch found himself in a long room full of colour. It looked like his garden in summertime, without the perfumes. All the cupboard doors had flowers painted on them.

There were also some pictures of castles which reminded him rather worryingly of the one he had seen on his ill fated trip to Romania. There were no daffodils; he knew these because he was always being told by Dad to 'Get off the daffodils.' He had thought this a little unfair because the daffodils didn't grow sensibly in the flower bed, but wandered all over the lawn where he was allowed to go for the rest of the year. But here in the floating house all of the interior seemed to be decorated with the pink, white and yellow flowers which he avoided because of their vicious thorns.

'Bright, isn't it,' said Brindley: 'My person does that with a brush and coloured stuff in a tin - I think it is because he can't bring our garden with him.'

As he gazed at the traditional roses and castles depicted on nearly every surface of the room, the warmth struck him and Patch could see a glowing wood-burning stove at the far end.

'Look what I've found,' the woman said to the man reading the newspaper by the fire.

'Good Heavens! What is it?'

'Don't be unkind, the poor little lad is wet through. He's either fallen or been thrown into the river. He was lucky to get out with it running so fast at the moment.'

'Odd-looking creature. I hope he wasn't thrown in because they may not want him back and, knowing you, you'll want to keep him. He looks a bit familiar actually.'

'I've got a perfectly good home with people who love me.' Patch told Brindley.

'I'm sure you have. Don't mind him, he says these things but he doesn't really mean it. He's always slipping me treats when she isn't watching.'

'Don't be horrid. And get me a towel,' said the woman. She led Patch over to the rug in front of the stove and rubbed him with the towel until he tingled all over. The man offered him a bowl of water. Patch turned his head away.

'I don't care if I never see water again,' he told Brindley; shivering as he remembered.

'He's still cold. Try some warm milk with a teaspoon of brandy in it,' suggested the woman. Patch sniffed the mixture. It smelled odd, but a tentative lap revealed that it tasted divine; he quickly lapped it up and licked the bowl, before looking expectantly up at the man.

'Shall I give him some more?' he asked.

'Better not. We don't want to be handing a pixilated dog back to his owner. I'll ring the police and see if anyone has reported him missing.'

It seemed that they had, and Dad was still out looking for him while Mum waited at home by the phone trying to comfort Jimmy.

Patch stretched out with Brindley on the rug in front of the stove, feeling a strange but very pleasant tingle as the brandy reached his bloodstream and began to flow around his body. His nose and his toes felt funny. When Dad arrived, having parked the car up by the bridge, Patch was sound asleep.

'I can't understand it,' Dad was saying: 'Patch is such a good dog. He's never tried to run away before. I think someone must have stolen him and he managed to escape from them, then found he was lost. Or perhaps they threw him in the river. Oh! Poor little lad.' Dad picked him up and hugged him which Patch found most embarrassing in front of Brindley.

97

'Don't worry. That's humans for you. It's well meant and we just have to put up with that kind of behaviour.'

Patch decided that Brindley was very wise. Much better to have him as a friend than quest-obsessed Gregory: 'We were going to Wales, you know,' he said.

'We went there once, it took about five weeks. Nice place, but a very long walk. What were you going to do for food?'

'I don't know. The dog I was going with didn't seem to have planned important things like that. The dog warden took him while I was in the river.'

'Are you going to try again?' asked Brindley.

'Most definitely not. I'm giving up excitement. It gets your feet bitten by rats,' he said, licking his sore toe.

Before Brindley could ask him to explain further, Dad picked him up, thanked Brindley's people and carried Patch to the car: 'I can still walk,' Patch said. But as usual Dad didn't hear.

He had to put up with more cuddling and even kissing when he got home, but it was all worth it when Mum produced a huge bowl of chicken. He'd known he was hungry but suddenly he was starving and he wolfed it down faster than he had ever eaten his supper, then, wonder of wonders, Mum filled his bowl up again. He finally waddled into his bed feeling very fat and lay listening to his family discussing his disappearance.

'He must have been stolen - Patch has never run away before,' said Mum.

'It was a 'spur of the moment' thing,' Patch beamed at them.

'Who would want to steal him? He's not the prettiest dog in the world,' said Dad.

Patch had to think about this. It was true he wasn't pretty, and didn't want to be, but Dad's remark held the implication that he was in some way unattractive. Before he had time to brood on this, Ankle-shredder's voice came into his head.

'Hello, Patch. Are you both in Wales yet?'

'No. The whole thing was a very bad idea. Gregory got dog-napped and I got flung into a raging torrent by a rat and almost drowned.'

'Sounds exciting! Now tell me what really happened, and where you are.'

'I'm at home.' He suddenly felt deeply tired: *'I'll tell you about it in the morning.'* Just before he fell asleep he wondered whether he should tell Gregory that he was now safe, then decided against it. He didn't want to get dragged into any more of the Sealyham's mad plans. Not being pack leader at home wasn't really so bad. It was a lot better than spending a cold night, soaking wet, suspended over a dangerous river full of toe-biting rats. He began to snore gently.

CHAPTER SEVEN

Patch woke as the sun, streaming through the kitchen window, warmed his back. He stretched luxuriously, then sneezed. For a moment he wondered whether he had caught some life-threatening disease from his immersion in the river, but as the sneeze didn't happen again he decided he was all right.

'Oh! Poor Patch. Have you caught a cold?' It was Mum coming into the kitchen to get breakfast ready.

Patch, seeing possible advantage to be gained, reacted swiftly and sneezed again. It wasn't such a convincing sneeze, more of a snort, really, but it brought the required result. Mum bent down beside his bed and put a hand on his head: 'Hm, you don't feel as if you have a temperature. I wonder what one gives a dog with a cold...I suppose honey and lemon is out.'

'Chicken,' Patch beamed at her.

'Are you hungry?' she asked.

For a moment he wondered if he had finally made a breakthrough and could actually connect mentally with his own humans. He tried again: *'Chicken.'* And for special effect he moved his short tail weakly against the side of his bed and put on what he thought was his most appealing expression.

Mum called Dad into the kitchen: 'Patch is looking peculiar,' she said: 'Do you think he's all right?'

'Maybe we should let the vet check him over,' said Dad: 'We don't know how long he was in the water and you can catch nasty illnesses from water. Rats spread Weils disease.'

'What kind of vile disease?'

' No. Weils disease, you pronounce the W as a V.'

Rats! Patch had a picture of Arvicola Terrestris rising in his mind. Harvey-thing, what did I ever do to you that you should infect me with a vile disease, he thought, then remembered that he didn't really feel ill at all. In fact he felt pretty good and as chicken didn't seem to be the cure for a cold, he let his face relax from the 'appealing' expression and got out of bed. He shook himself vigorously before walking to the back door and asking to be let out.

'I'll just watch him for a while,' said Mum.

Patch gave a little jump at the door to prove that he didn't need to see the vet and Dad let him out. As he crossed the lawn, Gregory's voice came into his head.

'Where are you, boy? Are you dead?'

He was tempted not to answer and let the Sealyham worry for a while.

'Patch, answer me. I've been trying to reach you all night. Who am I going to get to accompany me on my quest if you are dead? Oh, I don't know,' his voice took on a thoughtful tone: *'I could ask the gorgeous Ankle-shredder to take a holiday from her cows.'*

'Oh no! I'm not having that.' Patch hadn't meant this thought to travel.

'Got you, boy. Glad you're not dead. Very inconvenient that would have been. Where are you?'

'I'm at home, no thanks to you, and home is where I am staying.'

'No sense of adventure, some people,' said Gregory.

'It's your adventure. You go and have it.'

'I will, boy; soon as I can get out again. I'll keep in touch.'

Later that morning, Patch's family decided to have lunch at the pub on the green. There were plenty of tables outside and well-behaved dogs were welcome. They even tolerated Flash as long as he was muzzled and tied to something immovable.

Patch's heart did a little flutter as they walked across the village green and he saw Ankle-shredder lying in the shade under one of the tables, then a wave of jealousy swept over him as he realised that the white patch next to her was not her master's discarded cricket pullover, but a Sealyham-shaped dog.

'Hello, Annie,' said Patch.

'Hello, boy. You don't look too bad,' said Gregory.

'Why would he look bad?' asked Ankle-shredder.

'Well, I was about to tell you. He rather messed up my quest yesterday, you know.'

'How?'

'He had a good chance to catch a rat for supper, but instead he fell in the river and got stuck up a tree.'

'What! At the same time?' asked Ankle-shredder.

'Then he led me into getting trapped by the dog control officer.'

This was all so unfair that Patch just stared at him, speechless

'Don't worry, boy. I forgive you,' said Gregory.

This set the seal on Patch's speechlessness and he lay down on the other side of Ankle-shredder while he thought about something rude that he could say to Gregory. He curled his lip at the Sealyham and bared a few front teeth.

'You've got a piece of chicken stuck in your teeth,

boy,' said his rival.

Patch yawned as if he found Gregory the most boring dog on earth - which he actually did at that moment. To his surprise, Gregory yawned, then so did Ankle-shredder. He tried it again and, after a few moments, both the other dogs yawned. He felt better. I can control then both if I want to, he thought, settling down on the cool grass and feeling with his tongue for the trapped piece of chicken.

'As I was saying,' Gregory said, turning back to Ankle-shredder: 'You asked me earlier what Sealyhams do. Well, we are rather special dogs.'

'Of course,' Patch muttered.

They both ignored him.

Gregory continued: 'My mistress said, the other day, that there were only fifty-seven of us registered with the Kennel Club last year.'

'You may be special, but you are obviously not very popular with humans,' sneered Patch who had never been registered anywhere and wasn't likely to be.

Gregory ignored this and continued: 'My breed was developed many years ago by a human called Captain John Edwards of Sealyham Mansion. He wanted a really fierce terrier to work with his pack of hounds. My ancestors were Dandie Dinmonts and Cheshire Terriers. They had to go to ground after fox and badger and he wanted us white so that when we came back up, smelling of fox and badger, the hounds would realise we were not those animals and kill us by mistake.'

'How exciting,' said Ankle-shredder, her eyes sparkling.

'We used to be very popular with humans, years

ago. They kept us in their houses to catch rats. Then, I've heard, we got too popular and there were too many of us bred and we got a reputation for aggression.'

'Well, you'd need that for foxes and badgers,' said Ankle-shredder, a bit of aggression never bothered her.

'Granted,' said Gregory: 'But biting *people* doesn't go down so well.'

'Do you bite people?' she asked.

'No, girl. Never…can get you into a lot of trouble.'

'Patch bit someone once,' she said, remembering the Agility night at her farm.

'And what happened?' asked Gregory.

'It got me into a lot of trouble,' said Patch.

Mrs Collins stood up and tugged on Gregory's lead. He got unwillingly to his feet: 'Gotta go, you two. I'll let you know when I set out on the quest again. Annie, you'll be welcome to join me,' he said over his shoulder as he was pulled towards the car.

'Don't - he's insane,' said Patch.

'I think he's rather nice. His white hair compliments my black.'

'I'm white,' said Patch.

'Yes, but it's sort of interrupted by that black patch…Oh! Is that why they call you Patch?'

'Give that bitch a prize,' he said.

'Is that what Dachdan calls sarcasm?' she asked, with interest.

'I suppose so,'

'I can't do sarcasm, will you teach me?'

'It wouldn't suit you, you are perfect the way you are.'

'You are nice, Patch,' she said, nuzzling his ear and

104

making him feel quite frisky.

Patch's family were talking to their friends about his mysterious disappearance and possible abduction, when they were overheard by an eager young newspaper reporter at the next table. He introduced himself to them and told them that it sounded like a story for the local paper: 'Was it the pretty little black one?' he asked, peering under the table.

'No. Him', said Dad, pulling Patch out into the sunlight.

The reporter looked slightly disappointed: 'Is he a pedigree dog?' he asked, doubtfully, obviously wondering why anyone would want to steal Patch, who didn't really hear this exchange as he was still gazing with adoration at his beloved Annie.

'We'd need some pictures. Would you be prepared to take him back to the narrowboat where he was rescued, so that we could re-create the scene?'

'I expect so, if it is still there. A bit of publicity may stop some other poor dogs being stolen,' said Dad.

The reporter took out his mobile phone and spoke to the newspaper's photographer: 'She can be here in quarter of an hour, is that all right with you?'

Dad agreed, and told him about Patch's other excursions into the media which really excited the reporter as this gave quite another slant to the piece he was already writing in his head. The headline changed from 'Local dog lost, believed stolen' to 'Dramatic river rescue of Famous TV star'. With this title it might even reach the 'Nationals', he thought, going on to the sub-heading; 'Dog thieves brutally snatch Patch from his owner and try to end his career by drowning'. Feeling very excited now, he bent over

Patch and patted him on the head with a heavy hand. Patch ducked and pulled away back under the table.

'What was that about?' Ankle-shredder asked.

'They think I was stolen when I went with Gregory. Now I'm to be taken back to Brindley's house on the river.'

'Why? Who's Brindley?'

'I'm not sure why - I wasn't really listening, I was looking at you,' then he told her all about Brindley and his floating house of flowers.

It wasn't often that Patch had Ankle-shredder all to himself and he was basking in the luxury of it when she looked over his shoulder and gave a short double-bark: 'Dachdan!'

'Oh no,' Patch groaned as Ankle-shredder got up, tail wagging, to greet Dachdan.

'Hello,' said Patch, with a palpable lack of enthusiasm.

'I'm not speaking to you,' said Dachdan.

'Do I look bothered?' asked Patch.

'You couldn't have cared less about me being dragged off to the vet's yesterday.'

This was true: 'I was busy,' Patch drawled.

'He went on a quest with Gregory. We are lucky he is still alive,' said Ankle-shredder, giving Patch one of her soft, eyes-half-closed looks, which made his heart miss a beat. She didn't do 'soft' looks very often.

Dachdan sneered and looked away.

A car pulled up and parked on the side of the green and the driver came across to their table. It was the photographer.

'Is it the little black one...very photogenic,' she said.

'No, the white job,' said the reporter.

The photographer looked a bit disappointed.

'Come on, Patch.' Dad pulled him away from his love.

'Talk to you later, Annie,' said Patch, trying to return her soft look whilst being mildly strangled by his collar as he was towed towards the car.

'Come on, boy. You can see Dachdan some other time,' said Dad. Patch marvelled at the insensitivity and ignorance of humans.

They parked near the bridge and all set off along the towpath towards where the narrowboat had been moored. Dad unclipped Patch's lead, letting him trot on ahead. A high pitched squeak from the long grass beside the river caught his attention.

'I know what it is,' said Arvicola Terrestris: 'I've died and gone to hell. Whatever did I do that was so venial a sin that I should be punished thus?'

'You don't look very dead to me,' said Patch: 'Dead things are sort of flat. Not standing on their hind legs shrieking abuse at innocent passing dogs.'

'Innocent! Innocent! Vandal! Home-wrecker!'

Patch shook his head to try and relieve the strain on his vibrating eardrums.

'Everyone stand still,' whispered the photographer, rapidly taking shots of Arvicola Terrestris: 'It's a water vole. They're quite rare.' She studied the result on her digital camera: 'Lovely! Got some really good 'pics'. We'll try to work them into the story, somehow. You'd better call the dog away before he chases it.'

Chase it? I'm not *that* brave, Patch thought. Not only would I never hear the end of it, but I'd never hear the end of it in words I couldn't understand. The toe that the water vole had bitten, twice now, gave a slight twinge and he limped a couple of steps as he made his way back onto the path.

'Good riddance!' The squeak reached him, followed by a small splash. He turned and watched the vee-shaped wake travel across the river.

As they rounded the next bend they saw that the narrowboat had gone. There was some discussion as to whether they should search the river for it, but the photographer had been dragged away from her lunch and wasn't too keen: 'Write a piece about water voles to go with these pictures,' she told the reporter as they reached their cars.

'That's a shame,' Dad said to Patch as he lifted him into the back of the car: 'Now the water vole will be famous instead of you.'

He's welcome, Patch thought. He wanted to get back to Ankle-shredder.

But in this desire he was disappointed, as Dad drove straight past the pub and turned into their driveway.

'Where are you Annie?' Patch beamed.

'At home, in the barn, just doing a bit of 'ratting'. Oh! There's one.' Her thoughts switched off and Patch imagined her burrowing between the straw bales and chasing rats along their runs at the foot of the stone wall of the barn. He would have liked to join in the excitement, but would have probably left the actual rat-catching to Ankle-shredder, after all it would only have been polite...and he could still feel the twinge in his bitten toe.

CHAPTER EIGHT

It was several unremarkable days later that Gregory's thoughts came through to Patch as he sat in the garden watching a woodlouse cross the path

'I'm off again, boy. Thought I'd try getting a lift in a car, this time. Probably have more luck on my own. D'you mind?'

'Not at all. Good luck.' The woodlouse climbed onto the lawn and disappeared in the grass.

'I'll let you know how I get on.'

Although Gregory was no longer trying to contact him, Patch found he was getting vague impressions of the Sealyham's feelings. Sun-warmed tarmac under his paws. Then the comfortable feeling of letting warmth from the road seep into his belly. It seemed as if Gregory was lying down in the road. This didn't seem like a particularly sensible idea to Patch and while he was considering telling Gregory this, his sharp ears caught the faint squeal of skidding vehicle tyres far away in the distance.

'Hello, Gregory. Are you dead?' Even as he beamed this message Patch realised it was a stupid question because if Gregory had said 'yes', that would have meant he was in contact with a ghost, and Patch didn't like ghosts. He decided to wait and see if Gregory contacted him; hopefully still as a sentient being: 'Sentient! Did I really think that word,' he muttered. His mind drifted on wondering if the water vole's latest bite had infected him with whatever it was that caused it to use such impressive vocabulary. He'd done it again! Shaking his head to clear it, he got up and walked down to the garden gate where he sat looking out onto the village green.

After a few minutes a car stopped across the green and a man got out and went into the shop. A white head came up in the back of the car and watched the man though the window. The lady from the shop came out with the car driver and they both looked at the dog in the car. She shook her head and returned to the shop. The man got into the car and drove off. A bank of cloud began to drift across the sun.

'*I got a lift. I'm on my way, boy. Saw you watching.*'

'*I wasn't sure it was you,*' Patch said. He decided not to mention the fact that he had thought Gregory had been run over and, as a few spots of rain began to fall, he wandered back indoors. He had a slight antipathy towards getting wet, at the moment.

Half an hour later, as he was just beginning to think it was time for his five small lunch-time biscuits - Dad always seemed to think it was funny to say, 'Here Patch. Your fifteen biscuits.' Does he really think I am that stupid, thought Patch, who could count. Five was all paws and a tail. Fifteen was three dogs - Gregory came through again.

'*You there, Patch? This is proving more difficult than I thought.*'

'*What's the problem?*' Patch wasn't at all sure he wanted to hear it.

'*I'm in prison. In a cell at the police station. Horrible place, it reeks of human despair. They think I'm lost again and they've sent for the dog warden to take me home.*'

'*Will you give up now?*'

'*Never. I'll go back to walking. Don't suppose you want to join me again?*'

'*No thank you. But keep in touch,*' said Patch, one

eye on Mum who was heading towards the cupboard where his food was kept. She didn't play silly games with the biscuits.

'Here you are…your fifteen biscuits,' said Mum.

'Not you too,' this came out as a low, long-suffering growl.

'What's the matter? Don't you want them?'

'Yes, yes,' he wagged his tail, hoping against hope that she could count to three dogs. She counted out five biscuits onto his feeding mat. Two of them were the black charcoal ones which tasted like eating bonfires. He left them till last.

*

The sunshine woke him the next morning and as he yawned and stretched, Gregory's voice came into his head.

'She's just let me out. Lovely day for it. It has to be today because she is talking about a collar and identity disc. Says if I escape again I'll be returned immediately. I said goodbye to her…as usual she didn't notice. On reflection I shouldn't have said anything. She got the gardener to block up my escape route, but she doesn't know about the rotten fence post behind the rhododendrons. I can push the wire up there.'

'Nice day for questing,' said Patch: *'Stay clear of humans. They spoil all our fun.'* He got a faint impression of the feel and scent of damp leaf mould as Gregory squeezed under the fence.

Later that morning, as Patch and Dachdan were being walked on the common, Gregory came through again.

'I've reached the river, boy. Seem to have come on it a bit further up than where you went for a swim.'

111

Patch gave a little shiver and tried not to remember his near-death-experience.

'Was that that mad Sealyham?' asked Dachdan, catching the tail end of the message.

'Yes. He's on his way to Wales, again.'

'You don't often come across insanity in dogs, do you?' said Dachdan: 'Oh, except Flash...and that Chico.'

'That's front paws - and one hind if you add Gregory,' said Patch.

'What?'

'Never mind.'

'And Daffodil,' said Dachdan, looking nervously across the expanse of heather all around them.

'Nearly a whole dog,' Patch muttered.

Their two humans sat down on the bench at the top of the hill and gazed across the view of woods and fields to the Downs in the distance while they talked. Dachdan, who had made himself nervous by thinking of Daffodil, lay down under the bench. Patch scent marked a decaying birch log beside the path and stood watching a large green dragonfly as it snatched a small butterfly out of the air, nipped off its wings, and darted away carrying the body. Then he moved over to a rabbit hole in the bank. He could smell rabbits down there in the dark and barked for Dachdan to join him. But Dachdan had lost interest in rabbiting since he got trapped in a burrow for the night, and, according to him, nearly died.

The 'yelp' of a dog in distress, distracted Patch before he realised the sound had come from inside his head.

'Did you yelp, Gregory?' he beamed.

'I slipped down the bank. Nearly fell in. Can't see a

bridge anywhere. *What's that?'*

Patch waited a moment before beaming: *'What's what?'*

'A rat! It's arguing with me.' Gregory sounded horrified.

Patch sat down and concentrated really hard until he could hear both sides of the confrontation; he only knew one rat that was aggressive enough to stand up to a dog. Sure enough it was Harvey-thing.

'You're on my private beach. Get off! Dogs aren't allowed.'

Gregory was so surprised he was actually answering it: *'I don't really want to be on your beach. I slipped.'*

'Well go and slip somewhere else.'

'Not very friendly, are you?...considering I haven't eaten you...yet. I'm on a quest. Going to Wales. They are very friendly there and always keep a welcome - as long as you speak Welsh, of course.'

'Well I don't, so push off!'

'They keep a welcome in the hillside.'

'Are the Welsh known for obscure unintelligible remarks, as well?'

'You talk a lot for a rat.'

Oh, oh! thought Patch. Harvey-thing does not like being called a rat. Sure enough the water vole's answer came as an outraged scream.

'Rat! Rat! I'm a water vole. A protected species, so give up any idea of eating me or you'll be in deep trouble with the conservationists.'

'You there, Patch?' beamed Gregory.

'Yes.'

'What's a conservationist?'

'No idea.'

'This thing is threatening me with deep trouble and conservationists. 'Deep trouble' I know from last year. Deep trouble is what happens when you sit in the middle of the road, waiting for a lift to Wales, and cause a tractor to swing wide to avoid you, leaving no room for the car approaching from the other direction. Shut in for days, I was. Well, I don't think I can bother with this rat any more. I have to look for a bridge.' He addressed the water vole again: *'Right, rat. You tell me how to cross this river and I'll leave you alone.'*

'You use my proper name first...then I may tell you, just to get rid of you. My name is Arvicola Terrestris...say it.'

'All right, Harvey Terrorist. Where will I find a bridge?'

'That's not correct...Oh, I can't be bothered. Follow the river that way, there's a bridge...after that field of sheep. Now leave me in peace.'

'What's sheep?'

'Those white things...look a bit like you, only more attractive.'

After this exchange there was silence and Patch visualised Gregory trotting off along the tow-path. Dad and Dachdan's owner stood up and strolled on along the track. Patch shook his head, partly to dislodge the sand in his hair that he'd acquired whilst sticking his head into the rabbit burrow, but mostly to try to stop the ringing in his ears after hearing the water vole's high-pitched tirade. He vaguely wondered why it was only himself that Harvey-thing had bitten...twice.

'Are you coming?' asked Dachdan emerging from his, hopefully Daffodil-proof, lair under the seat.

The two men turned and whistled for their dogs to catch up.

'I don't know how to tell you this,' said Dachdan, as they trotted side by side along the heather fringed track.

'What?' asked Patch, skirting a puddle he would normally have splashed through.

'I'm coming to live with you.'

'WHAT?' Patch skidded to a halt, facing Dachdan.

'I heard them talking, something about a holiday and I'm coming to your house.'

'What's wrong with Kennels? That's where dogs usually go when their people have holidays.'

'Very welcoming,' sneered Dachdan.

'You're not having my bed, or my biscuits…except the black ones; you can have those,' Patch said, feeling quite magnanimous for a second.

'I'm not going to enjoy this any more than you,' said Dachdan. In a strange way their mutual antipathy united them for the next few yards.

*

It was half an hour after Patch had got home when Gregory came through again.

'I need help, boy.'

Patch thought about not answering, he had no intention of getting involved with Gregory's daft quest again.

'Patch. Where are you?' Gregory sounded scared.

Patch got a strong smell of sheep with this message, and he remembered Harvey-thing's last directions to Gregory. Had he been attacked by a sheep on his way to the bridge? Was he lying injured in the field? He tried to ignore these thoughts but it didn't work. He sighed.

'What's happened?' he beamed reluctantly.

'I'm trapped.'

'Trapped where, and by what? If you've fallen in the river you can stay trapped, after you abandoned me there, the other day.'

'No, sorry about that. No, I'm trapped in a box. I was crossing this field, see. With these sheep things in it and they all started to run at me. There was a collie dog chasing them - very rude he was. Told me to get out of the way. So I did. There was this enormous dark box in the field, so I ran up a ramp and hid at the end, but then all the sheep came and hid in there with me...and somebody has shut the door. Now the box is moving, it is some kind of vehicle, and I'm going to be trampled to death by all these sharp hooves. Ouch!'

'What do you expect me to do?'

'I don't know. Ouch! Get off!' Gregory switched off.

'Are you there, Gregory?' There was no answer.

For the next four hours Patch received intermittent cries for help from Gregory, which was very inconvenient as his after-lunch snooze was constantly interrupted and he was getting tired of the smell of sheep. Also, it wasn't leaving his mind free to worry, seriously, about having to share his home with Dachdan.

*

'I'm free, boy. I'm free.' This joyous scream in his head woke Patch from a deep sleep on the sitting room rug where, until he had 'dropped off', he had been watching television with his family.

Bother, he thought, I've missed nearly all of 'The Dog Whisperer'. He needed to watch this programme

116

to be prepared for all the totally unnecessary control techniques that Jimmy might practise on him over the next few days. Patch had no intention of becoming a noisy, destructive and dangerous 'red-zone' dog. It would waste far too much energy.

'Where are you?' he asked Gregory.

'You're not going to believe this, boy. Have a guess.'

Patch looked at the tail end of the programme on the television: 'America,' he beamed.

'Why would I be in America?'

'So that The Dog Whisperer could train you to stop running away.'

'Don't know what you're talking about. I'm in Wales...in Sealyham! I've just escaped from the lorry, so have the sheep, they've run away in a field. I heard the farmer tell the driver that this was Sealyham. I've done it...my Quest.'

'What are you going to do now?'

'Look for some of my relations. I'll let you know how I get on.' Gregory switched off.

Patch realised he hadn't asked him how he was going to get home again...then decided he didn't really care, and went back to sleep.

CHAPTER NINE

Dachdan had been at Patch's house for three days. Three days of utter misery for both of them. Trying to be polite to each other was proving to be a great strain. It had rained solidly for those three days and Dad, who had a cold, had put off taking them for a walk. This hadn't bothered Patch particularly because he was still averse to any water that wasn't in his drinking bowl, but Dachdan had kept up a continuous moan about how he was afraid of losing his figure due to the lack of exercise. Patch couldn't see how having the most ravishing figure in the world would compensate for Dachdan's ugly head and finally said so, to shut him up. This had resulted in a small, undignified scuffle in the kitchen, since which neither had spoken to the other.

When Gregory came through again it was a relief to both of them as they then had something else to occupy them, other than sitting in their respective beds glaring at each other.

'Patch...I need your help. I'm in prison and I need to get out.'

'Tell me about it,' said Patch, with a sly look at Dachdan.

'Cuts both ways,' Dachdan snapped, having heard both sides of the telepathic conversation.

'I will tell you about it,' said Gregory, misunderstanding Patch's meaning: *'Getting on all right, I was, until this woman caught me as I was talking to one of my relatives that she had on a lead. She took me to a police station...Welsh police stations aren't any nicer than English ones. They both have a sickening smell of distressed humans in*

118

the cells. I had to put up with that for a while and then another woman came and took me to a dog prison. It's not fair. I never done nothing. She says I'm in Sealyham rescue, whatever that is. There's a couple of other dogs here, they're not happy either. I didn't need rescuing, but I do now. Tell you the truth, boy, I am a bit fed up with my quest...I mean, I got here didn't I? And now I think I would like to go home.'

'What can I do from here?' Patch asked.

'Why don't you go and fetch him, leave me in peace for a bit,' said Dachdan.

'May I remind you that this is *my* house. If anyone is to leave, it should be you...and the sooner the better,' said Patch.

'Are you receiving me, Patch?'

'Yes, but I don't see what I can do. Leave it with me. I'll try and think of something.'

'Well hurry up. I hate it here.'

'Serves him right,' said Dachdan.

At that moment, Dad came into the kitchen carrying their leads: 'It's stopped raining, boys. Let's get out.' Both dogs rushed towards him wagging their tails.

Dad led them out into a morning washed clean and fresh by the heavy rain. The sun came out and the road surface began to steam as he led them down towards the bridge. As they slipped down the muddy slope to the towpath along the riverbank, Dachdan looked nervously downstream, prepared for instant flight if Daffodil appeared from that direction again.

'Daffodil's all right, as long as you don't show any fear or aggression...do what the Dog Whisperer says and fill yourself with calm assertive energy,' said

119

Patch.

'And how do you do that when you are terrified?'

'I don't know, actually, but it sounds good.'

A mallard duck quacked in the rushes beside them, making Dachdan shy away from the edge of the path, and as he looked towards the sound, he saw something else: 'What's that?...in the water.'

Patch picked out a small brown head, bobbing in mid-stream: 'It looks like another of those water vole things that aren't rats...or it's a rat.'

The water vole was swimming frantically to avoid being swept away by the rushing water, a swirling eddy pushed it in to the bank below them and it pulled itself out onto the shore. Then it saw the dogs. For half a second it contemplated diving back into the water, then it recognised Patch.

'You again!' it squeaked.

'I think it's that Harvey thing,' said Patch: 'Weren't you supposed to be on your way to Oxford?'

'If you were remotely in touch with nature you would have been able to understand that heavy rain creates swollen rivers, producing huge navigational dangers to those who are somewhat challenged by their lack of size, and who are desirous of pursuing a journey *upstream*.'

'Why don't you walk?' asked Dachdan, reasonably.

'Because I am liable to meet ugly monsters like you,' said the water vole.

'And get eaten,' said Dachdan, pouncing towards him. Then pouncing back as he nearly fell in.

'Dogs! What good are you?' the water vole shrieked above the sound of the rushing water: 'You are nothing but manipulative parasites, preying on humans for your food and shelter. What do you give in return? Nothing! You control them to gain your own ends.'

Dachdan answered him: 'What we give is that we fulfil their desire to be controlled.'

Patch thought that this was quite profound, coming from Dachdan. And, as he thought more about it, he realised that even he could, occasionally, make his people do what he wanted. And they did provide him with a warm, comfortable bed and regular food, not quite enough chicken, but he resolved to give that problem some serious consideration. In return for this he wondered what *he* did. Nothing, he concluded, but then this was what Dachdan had just said. A dog only had to be a dog; that seemed to be enough for most humans. Pursuing this thought, he found a flaw…Ankle-shredder worked for the farmer who owned her…but then continuing this thought further, he realised that Ankle-shredder only really worked for herself as she loved chasing and biting the cows' heels.

'Are you going to sit there looking weird, all day?' Dachdan asked.

Patch stood up and shook himself. He saw that the water vole had gone: 'You haven't eaten it, have you?' he asked.

'Not much good at multi-tasking are you? It is possible to think with your eyes open, you know. No, of course I haven't eaten it, I thought it looked pretty indigestible, full of all those long words as it is. Besides, I think I might miss exchanging insults with it.'

'And you call me weird,' said Patch. With a last

glance at the water which looked extremely dangerous to him, he set off after Dachdan who had nearly caught up with Dad.

A series of short, sharp barks came from the field behind the hedge on the other side of the towpath…Ankle-shredder!

'Hello, Annie,' he beamed. *'I can hear you.'*

'Can't talk now, Patch. I'm working… Bark! Bark! Move, you great stupid beast,' she shouted at a difficult cow, who was staring round, trying to see where the noise was coming from: *'Patch. My person says that when I have got these cows into the barn we are going to that place in the village where the humans gather to drink that disgusting beer stuff. Will you be there?'*

'We'll try to drag Dad in that direction on the way back from our walk…shouldn't be too difficult.'

'Who's we?'

'Dachdan is staying with me.'

'I hope you are being nice to each other.'

'Sort of. Hope to see you later.'

'That was Annie,' said Patch, catching up with Dachdan and Dad.

'I heard. You didn't exactly tell her the truth about our relationship.'

'Well, you know Annie likes her friends to be happy.'

'Hmmph,' said Dachdan, blowing out his cheeks.

*

The pub was busy with lunch-time customers when they arrived. Ankle-shredder was already there, trying to explain the finer points of cow-herding to young Nell, who was gazing admiringly at her.

Letitia was deep in conversation with a lady that

122

Patch didn't know. The lady was handing out leaflets about her lost dog and he heard the name Gregory mentioned. This must be his owner, Mrs. Collins.

'It's that Gregory. She says he is lost,' said Ankle-shredder.

'No. He's in a prison called 'Sealyham Rescue'. He got to Wales, you know…but now they won't let him come back,' said Patch.

'He's an idiot!' said Dachdan.

'Don't be horrid, I thought he was nice. Very brave and positive,' said Ankle-shredder.

'Getting locked up in prisons all the time doesn't sound very positive to me,' Dachdan muttered. They ignored him.

Letitia was quietly telling Mrs. Collins that she had once used her powers as a clairvoyant to help the police find a lost person, and suggesting that she might be able to help her find Gregory. They arranged to meet that evening. Remembering that he had once managed to influence Madame Letitia, though not quite in the way he had expected, Patch pricked up his ears. Maybe he could help Gregory…without ever having to leave home and risk drowning again.

*

Later that evening, with Dachdan sound asleep in the other bed, Patch tried, unsuccessfully, to tune in to Madame Letitia. He thought for a minute, then tried to get through to Nell. It took a minute or two, then she came through, yawning and sounding very sleepy: *'What's the matter, Patch? I was nearly asleep.'*

'Sorry. Is your person alone?'

'No. That Gregory's person is here. They are in the

123

other room staring at a glass bowl on the table. I have been sent to bed for being too friendly.'

'Thank you, Nell...go back to sleep.'

'Oh. What's wrong with 'friendly'?

'Nothing, Nell. Humans are strange creatures, they never seem to know what they want. I will explain when I see you. Go to sleep.'

He sat up in his bed and concentrated really hard. Finally, and faintly, Madame Letitia's voice and thoughts came through. *'Is there anybody there?'*

Patch tried to contact Gregory, with no luck, but then he remembered that sometimes it helped to be higher up to achieve the range. He left the kitchen and went to the top of the stairs. It took a minute to raise Gregory as he, too, was asleep, but finally he came through. Patch explained that he might be able to help him and asked how he could explain to Madame Letitia where he was.

'Tell her that through a crack in the side of the big box on the way here, I could see a huge river. I think we went over it on a very high bridge. I am with two other Sealyhams here in this prison.'

'Be quiet now. I'm trying.' Patch beamed this information into Madame Letitia's mind.

'Something's coming through,' he heard her say to Mrs. Collins: *'I'm getting a bridge over a river. I see him with some of his own kind over the water.'*

Mrs Collins got a muddled impression of a 'doggy heaven' and asked if Gregory was dead.

'Tell her 'Wales', said Gregory, picking up the conversation through Patch's mind.

'Wales,' Patch beamed.

'Whales,' said Madame Letitia.

'Whales! Water? This doesn't make sense,' said

124

Mrs Collins.

'Send her 'Sealyham', said Gregory.

Patch tried again: *'Sealyham.'*

'Seal and Ham,' said Madam Letitia, in a puzzled tone.

'Whales, water, seals...ham? Has he been stolen and taken abroad on a ship?' asked Mrs Collins.

'This isn't working,' Patch beamed to Gregory.

'Don't give up, boy. One more time. Try 'Sealyham Rescue.'

Patch concentrated again.

'Seal and Ham rescue?' said Madame Letitia, sounding dreadfully confused.

Finally, Mrs Collins' brain engaged the right gear. *'Sealyham Rescue! Why didn't I think of that? Oh! thank you, thank you.'*

Patch gave a huge sigh. Concentrating for so long in two directions was an enormous strain.

'Patch. What's happening?'

'I think you are going to be rescued. I'm tired now.' He fell asleep, and the rest of Gregory's questions didn't get through. Neither did anything else until Jimmy tripped over him on the landing as he made his way to the bathroom. Patch got told off and sent back to his bed in the kitchen.

Dachdan woke up: 'What have you been up to, then?' he asked, enjoying watching Patch get into trouble.

'I'm probably the most misunderstood dog in the world,' said Patch, flopping down in his bed and immediately falling asleep again.

*

The next day, Patch and Dachdan were dozing off their morning walk in the sitting room, half listening to Mum and Dad talking.

'It seems Mrs Collins is off to Wales,' said Dad: 'Apparently she telephoned Sealyham Rescue and they told her they had three dogs looking for homes.'

Oh no! thought Patch, don't let her come back with three Gregorys. He wondered whether they had all been on a quest.

'She looked a bit embarrassed when she told me that Letitia had gazed into her crystal ball and told her that one of them was Gregory,' said Dad.

'I should think so,' said Mum: 'It can't be her dog. How on earth would he have got to Wales?'

'Not just to Wales…right across to west Wales, place called Sealyham, would you believe?'

'Sounds very odd to me. I wonder about that Letitia, you know. She claims to get messages from the spirit world, thinks she is in contact with King Charles,' said Mum.

It's me, actually,' Patch beamed at her, but she didn't notice.

She went on: 'No. It can't be Gregory. One Sealyham looks more or less like another. Bit like Dachdan there, only prettier and white.'

'Now your family have started insulting me, too,' grumbled Dachdan: 'I'll be glad to get home tomorrow.'

'Can't say I have enjoyed having you,' said Patch.

'D'you want a fight!' Dachdan growled.

'That's a thought,' said Patch: 'If we fight you won't have to come and stay here again.'

'Suits me,' said Dachdan: 'Where shall we have it?'

'Here; in the sitting room. The floor's a bit slippery in the kitchen - we don't want to get hurt.'

126

'Right. Lots of noisy snarling and growling and some fur-biting, but no blood,' said Dachdan.

Patch stood up and walked, menacingly over to Dachdan, his stumpy tail stuck up in the air and a ridge of hair raised along his spine, imagining he was a dangerous 'red zone' dog from one of the 'Dog Whisperer' programmes. Dachdan snarled and stood up. Patch pounced on him. Dachdan whipped round and grabbed Patch's leg. Patch screamed: 'You said no blood - let go, that hurts.'

Mum and Dad threw themselves into the fray and somehow Mum's hand got into Dachdan's mouth as she tried to remove Patch's leg. She yelled. Patch, meantime, had got hold of Dachdan's ear and it was Dachdan's turn to shriek. Dad pulled Patch away from Dachdan without first detaching him from the ear which began to bleed profusely.

In less than a minute this, supposedly painless, fight had left two dogs and one human dripping blood on the cream-coloured sitting room carpet.

Dad was furious: 'Right! Patch started that, so he is banished to the shed.' He picked him up and carried him out of the room.

Dachdan took himself back into the kitchen, leaving a trail of blood across the floor to his bed. He shook his head and the torn ear flap sprayed blood up the wall, and across his throat, which looked as if it had been cut.

'My leg is bleeding!' said Patch to Dad as he pushed him and his bed into the shed. Dad noticed the blood, inspected the leg, said: 'You'll live.' And slammed the shed door.

'That went well, didn't it,' said Dachdan: *'Got any more bright ideas?'*

'*Shut up!*' said Patch: '*You didn't stick to our agreement.*'

'*They'll probably have you 'put down' now, as a dangerous dog,*' sneered Dachdan.

'*It wasn't me that bit Mum. Think on that!*'

Dachdan went quiet and began to lick up the drops of blood from his torn ear.

The shed smelt of creosote which made Patch sneeze. He hoped he wouldn't be in there for too long because the noxious fumes could seriously damage his sense of smell. His discomfort was slightly mollified by picking up a shocked thought from Dachdan as Dad said he would take him to the vet to get his ear stitched: 'Don't want to hand him back even uglier,' Dad said as he led a complaining Dachdan out to the car.

When they had gone, Mum came and let him out and he bounced gratefully around her, trying to make up for upsetting her and explaining about the plan which had gone wrong.

'Get down! Patch. You are not forgiven. It's just that the shed smells a bit strong at the moment. I wouldn't like to spend much time in there. We'll shut you in the spare bedroom when Dachdan comes back.'

Good, he thought. I won't have to listen to him grizzling all night.

CHAPTER TEN

The two dogs were not left alone together again until Dachdan was picked up by his people. They didn't seem particularly upset by the fact that he had three stitches in his ear flap, especially as Dad had insisted on paying the vet's bill: 'That's no chicken for Patch for about a year, until he has paid for it,' he had joked.

This was no joke to Patch who instantly wished he had done Dachdan some serious damage - and might still if he got the chance.

The next time they met was outside the pub a few days later when most of the village dog-owners got together for a lunch-time drink. They ignored each other, which Patch found easy as Ankle-shredder was there and he only had eyes for his beautiful dark-haired lady. She was concentrating on him too, as Dachdan was still sulking. Flash was there but nobody ever took too much notice of Flash as his attention span was about three seconds, which didn't leave a lot of time for civilized conversation.

Suddenly Ankle-shredder's eyes were distracted from Patch to something behind him: 'Look who it is!' she barked.

Patch turned and saw Gregory and Mrs Collins walking across the green towards them.

'Hello, boy. Thank you for getting me out of that prison. I will always be grateful and I am really impressed at your ability to connect with humans.'

'Oh, it was nothing,' said Patch, acting embarrassed but secretly pleased that somebody had praised him in front of Ankle-shredder.

129

'It was 'touch and go' for a while there though, boy. She picked out one of the others; said it looked just like me. Changed her mind though when it was pointed out to her that the other two were bitches and she'd said she wanted a dog. She really doesn't think I am Gregory...can't believe I actually got that far. I am having to get used to being called 'Jimmy', and she says she hopes I will be friends with Gregory when he is found. It's doing my head in a bit. I might have to run away again, when I can decide where to go.'

The wind gusted across the green and swirled an empty crisp packet against Flash's ear as he dozed beside Dachdan. He woke instantly and pounced on Dachdan, hitting him on his sore ear with his muzzle. The muzzle saved Dachdan from lasting damage but didn't stop him screaming. Ankle-shredder gave him a nip, to stop the noise, as his owner dragged him away and shut him in the car.

Flash's owner hit his dog, tied him up to the fence, away from the others and went to buy everyone a drink.

Gregory studied Flash for a minute: 'There are some dogs in this village, ought to be in therapy,' he said: 'Not to mention their owners.' This last remark was prompted by the sight of his owner standing up to greet Letitia and Nell.

'Hello, you lot, have I missed the fun,' said Nell, breathlessly, wagging her tail at everyone: 'I heard some screaming. Why is Flash trying to hang himself from that fence?'

'Ignore him,' said Patch: 'Everyone else does.'

Nell touched noses, shyly, with Gregory: 'Patch rescued you, didn't he? I heard him talking to my person in the night.'

'Yes, and I'm deeply grateful. He will be my friend for ever. I am hoping he will come on my next adventure…when I have had a bit of a rest.'

Patch shuddered. I don't think so, he thought, but kept this thought to himself.

'How exciting!' said Ankle-shredder, eyes shining: 'Can I come?'

Well, maybe it could be fun, Patch re-thought, beaming adoration at his love, who was gazing at Gregory. A wave of jealousy swept over him until she turned and said: 'I can come, can't I Patch?'

'Of course you can, Annie.'

She nuzzled his ear and made the hair on his neck tingle.

'And me?' said Nell.

'Maybe when you are a bit older,' said Ankle-shredder.

Flash had stopped struggling and was sitting like a statue, his eyes fixed on the house where the short-tailed cat lived. His owner appeared with a tray of 'peace-offering' drinks for his friends.

In Patch's world everything was coming right. Dachdan was out of his house. He had successfully rescued Gregory who was back with them - he would have to give a bit more thought as to whether that *was* actually a good thing, but it meant that Ankle-shredder thought he was a hero and she was sitting very close beside him, the sunlight turning her black coat into an iridescent blue/black. He sighed with contentment. Yes, everything was wonderful.

The End.